THE HAUNTING OF THE ABERDEEN ESTATES

MASON DEAN

APRIL-MAY 2005

*J*onathan and Teresa Thompson lived on a secluded, sprawling estate just outside the official confines of the small village of Green Pond, South Carolina, with their two children, Katie, age seven, and Adam, age six. Based on their lives so far, Green Pond was a drastically different life-style, but both professional and personal circumstances had arisen for both of them. Life in the fast-paced, urban setting of New York City was beginning to wear on Teresa and Jonathan. The inherent dangers and temptations of the streets were making them have more than their normal level of concern for the kids as they grew up.

Jonathan had built and nurtured a very successful career in the financial services sector, both as an employee of a large firm and then one of his own when he had left the security of the corporate umbrella. He simply woke one day, realizing he no longer had the fire, drive, or ambition to continue. His once total dedication and passion for his chosen work was making him feel bored and empty inside. Despite the extremely lucrative life it had provided for them all, Jonathan was simply no longer enamored with the path he found himself on and knew a change was needed before he made himself miserable and depressed beyond recovery.

After talking it over with Teresa, he pulled the corporate plug on his life and moved the family from New York City to the rural setting of Green Pond. They had more than enough money to live on for a long time to come, and Jonathan just wanted a more relaxed and calmer way of life. When he came across an old, historic mansion on a huge acreage outside Green Pond, he knew he had found the perfect place in which to begin enjoying the fruits of his labors. The mansion, which had been sitting shuttered and vacant for some years, needed some serious TLC, but he saw great potential in the impressive and imposing property tagged "Aberdeen Estates" on an old, weathered, and chipped wooden sign at the entrance.

As for Teresa, she had been a stay-at-home mom once Katie and Adam had come along, and she was fully on board with the plan, thrilled the kids would be growing up in a more secure and protective rural setting than the mean streets of New York. Once they got relocated and settled in as much as was reasonable, considering the condition of the place, Jonathan hired a recommended general contractor, Tony Longmore, to step in and oversee what was likely to be a long and protracted renovation to meet the vision that Jonathan had for their new home. It was a bit of a concession in comfort for Teresa, relative to their luxury apartment up north, but the kids seemed to love the wide-open spaces, and she knew the living arrangements were just temporary.

Longmore moved ahead on the project at once with great excitement and eagerness as work in and around Green Pond was becoming a bit thin just then with a recent dip in the local economy. He got living quarters for the family taken care of right away, and once that was finished, he sat down with Jonathan. Together they mapped out a priority schedule for everything else to be brought back to life. And for a time, that was all that really went on in their lives. Adam and Katie had been home-schooled back in NYC under Teresa's very able tutelage, and that continued for the few weeks remaining in what would be a regular school term for the children.

While she oversaw the kids, Jonathan did, in fact, begin a life of relaxation and ease. He got more involved in Adam and Katie's lives, which he had not had the luxury of before, due to his obligations with his business. And he and Teresa found more time to spend together as well, which felt like a gift from above for both of them. In those early days, Jonathan never had a single regret about his decision to walk away and leave his financial consulting career behind. From outward appearances, it was a perfect family life for all four of them.

* * *

BUT THEN ONE DAY, out of the blue, in a manner very similar to that in which Jonathan had awoken to find he was no longer so interested in managing his clients' investments anymore, he was finding all the free time he now had on his hands no longer enough to give him the peace of mind he had thought would just naturally flow with the change in scenery. He loved Teresa and the kids, but he had never experienced so much idle time in all his adult life, and he did not know what to do with himself. Jonathan realized he did not really have any hobbies, nor did he have any interest in golf, tennis, or any other sporting activity that so many of his former colleagues had been consumed with.

Jonathan did not want to go back to his old ways, but to keep himself balanced and sane, he knew he had to find something else to add to his life to feel active and functional. The people of Green Pond were friendly and wonderful to be around, but for Jonathan, he needed more. He supposed the hustle and bustle of NYC were still in his blood, and life here overall was just too slow. He needed some intellectual challenge to fill in the gaps, but what that might be was a mystery. However, after calling some former colleagues and doing some research, Jonathan came up with a plan that would allow him to enjoy the slower pace and peace Green Pond had to offer while still keeping his brain engaged and his inner ambitions satisfied.

The timing seemed perfect, as Tony Longmore had the renovation project well in hand, and there was little, if anything, Jonathan could add to be of any assistance to him. He knew as much about renovation and construction as he did nuclear physics and was smart enough to let real professionals do what they were good at. He filled Tony in on his plans, and they both agreed that as long as Jonathan was easily reachable by phone, text, or email, then it should not be an issue as setting up this new enterprise, Jonathan told him, was going to require a bit of travel away from Green Pond.

Teresa said nothing in regard to this new venture. Without any discussion, she could see from his behavior of late that her husband needed more intellectual stimulation and a new challenge. She had never understood what he did before. The technical aspects of it were just a bit over her head. Quite frankly, anything in that field just bored her, and she assumed it was likely this new gig would be more of the same. After a lengthy discussion telling her that what he wanted to launch would initially require a lot of overnight travel away from Green Pond, Teresa assured him that was not an issue.

After all, she said, "It's not like Green Pond is New York City…."

She made it clear that she was plenty capable of taking care of the kids and herself in his absence. If anything serious arose, she was sure Tony would step in if needed. And with that pact in place, Jonathan set off on his new venture, promising to always be available to return immediately if she changed her mind or had something arise that she felt uncomfortable having Tony help her with.

MAY-JUNE 2005

*B*ack in Green Pond, while Jonathan was away, trying to convince new partners to join him in his new somewhat-risky enterprise, Teresa did indeed hold down the fort. She did not want it to sound indelicate or insulting but having Jonathan out from underfoot some days was a blessing. She was grateful he had found a new outlet for his bottled-up energy as she could see his growing ennui and frustration in the isolation and seclusion of Aberdeen Estates grinding on him. He was just not used to not having a regular schedule or a defined daily routine, and she had been afraid if this had not come along that he might snap. She loved Jonathan, but some days he had been getting on her nerves.

And as they had both hoped, Tony and his crew were always there if any need arose during what were becoming more frequent trips away from home. And blessedly, so far, nothing had been required of their contractor other than the normal idiosyncrasies that popped up occasionally due to ongoing renovations—electrical outages, water leaks, that kind of thing. Teresa had been able to handle it all, and she was proud of her ability to step up and take a much bigger role in their family responsibilities than ever before.

When Jonathan came home between trips, it was a wonderful and exciting reunion. Though a very tortured analogy, Teresa was finding it very similar to having him come home each day from work when they had lived in NYC, granted a bit longer in this case. When Jonathan had initially pitched his idea to her, she had been a bit reluctant, not so sure being apart so much of the time would be good for their relationship. She really had not anticipated that reaction when the arrangement was set up, but Teresa was finding their new lives better than ever.

But a few weeks later, a new wrinkle began to appear in the fabric of their lives which had nothing to do with Jonathan and his new business endeavors. Day by day, Tony found it harder and harder to keep a full crew at work at the mansion, despite the lack of other available opportunities in the area. He initially thought it was just some kind of twisted move to squeeze more money out of him since they knew Jonathan was wealthy and wanted the mansion wrapped up as soon as possible. It was an underhanded strategy, but Tony had seen that type of thing go on before, and right now, times were tough financially in Green Pond. But when Tony began to ask around among the few men still on the job site, he found out it had nothing to do with some strong-arm tactic to get more money out of him.

Partially, it was the remote and isolated location of Aberdeen Estates since most of his guys had limited means of transportation, often relying on one another for rides to and from the site. But when Tony dug deeper, he found that a number of the workers had gotten wind of the local legend he knew of well that had been passed down over time—the belief that the mansion was haunted. Tony thought the old tale utter nonsense and had been hopeful that word of it would not get to his guys, though even if it did, he assumed they would laugh it off as he did. These were lower-middle-class working men, and Tony just figured they were as filled with common sense and highly skeptical about such lore as he was, but apparently, he was wrong.

The word coming back to him was that several of the guys had begun to hear and see weird things on the job site, especially when the sun was nearly gone or had just set for the day. They were convinced it was evidence that the legend was more than just a myth. No matter how hard he pleaded with them and guaranteed them it was all just in their collective imaginations, Tony soon found himself with just a bare-bones crew that was now limping along in their progress relative to how quickly they had been humming along. Even the offer of substantial bonus pay to overcome their fears was wasted breath. The men abandoning the site soon told others around Green Pond of the haunted old mansion outside town, and even new recruits could not be found.

Tony himself stayed on, though, with just a few

others who did not believe in such things. He had never backed out of a contract with a client in his professional life. He explained the situation to Jonathan but assured him that work would go on, but perhaps at a fraction of the speed it had been happening. Unfortunately, their target date for completion was going to be drastically shoved back. Jonathan was obviously disappointed but just shrugged it off, telling Tony to do the best he could with the men who stayed on, promising an incentive bonus for Tony and the remaining crew. Jonathan figured it would be done when it was done, and he was not really hard-pressed to have the renovations completed by any set date anyway.

Tony thanked him for his understanding and patience, and work went on, just at a slower pace. Days went by, and late spring rolled over into summer in Green Pond, and the days lengthened in response easing any anxiety that Teresa had when the crew's numbers dropped off. Fewer nighttime hours made her less concerned about things at the house when Jonathan was away. She was not especially worried as she had seen no evidence of any problems for their security since they had arrived…and telling herself this was rural South Carolina and not NYC helped. Tony even offered to have himself or one of his remaining guys stay on-site overnight when Jonathan was gone, but Teresa politely refused his kind offer, seeing it as completely unnecessary. She was capable of taking care of her kids on her own.

* * *

BUT ONE HORRIBLE night in late June, that all changed. A tropical storm that had been brewing in the Caribbean, just off the coast of Cuba, began to move northward and slid up the eastern coast of the Carolinas. Growing up in central Virginia and then living in NYC, Teresa had never dealt with the hurricane-like storms the eastern seaboard had every season. To add to the iffy situation, Jonathan had just left for a trip in Chicago before the tropical depression made its move out of the Caribbean. Tony and his crew had been unable to work for almost two days by then due to the weather since their remaining work was all outside.

Tony had offered to have a guy stay with her during the onslaught, but Teresa knew how thinly stretched Tony was with his other jobs and felt silly having him dedicate a man just to ease her girlish fears. But as the winds picked up and the rain lashed the roof and sides of the mansion, Teresa suddenly wished she had taken him up on his offer. But she had not, and now it was too late. She just held it together as best she could, not wanting her own anxieties to be picked up by Adam and Katie and make them all totally freaked out. Teresa figured as long as the mansion itself stayed intact, she would be fine. She would just ride this thing out...*I mean, isn't it what seasoned residents here do all the time anyway?* It would not last forever, and when it was over, Tony and his guys would be back to patch up any wounds.

And for a few hours, Teresa was fine, and she went

to bed after putting Adam and Katie to bed as well. The noise from the wind whipping around the edges of the mansion was hideous as it thrashed the tall trees nearby, but otherwise, she was doing pretty good, she told herself. Just as Teresa had nodded off, a deafening clap of thunder shook the house and woke her rudely. She sat up and gasped as she got her bearings. Knowing she needed to check on the kids to make sure that massive explosion had not scared them too badly, Teresa reached over to turn on the lamp on the bedside table. But a series of clicks gave her no light.

She glanced into the bathroom and saw that the small nightlight she left on there to help her see if she had to get up in the middle of the night was out as well. *Great,* Teresa said to herself, *now the power is out as well.* She supposed it should not have surprised her based on the storm's ferocity, but it was aggravating all the same. She sat still, waiting for her heart to stop pounding so hard as she tried to figure out just how she was going to maneuver her way around in the dark. *If the kids do not cry out for help, does she really need to get up anyway? What exactly is she going to do...snap her fingers and summon the lights back on by magic?* Teresa had almost resigned herself to just waiting until daylight when her next move was made for her. She heard some strange crashing commotion coming from downstairs. Sitting tight was no longer an option.

JUNE 2005

*T*eresa felt her way along the hallway until she reached a small table on one side where she remembered they had stashed a flashlight for emergencies. She flicked it on, and it gave her just enough light to navigate down to the kids' bedrooms. Not surprisingly, they were both wide awake and huddled together in Katie's bed, trembling, their eyes wild with fright. Teresa went over and put a reassuring hand on each of them.

"It's okay, guys…just a storm passing by," Teresa said in a calm voice that belied her inner anxiety.

"What was that?" Adam squeaked out as he held fast to his big sister.

"Just thunder, honey…let's get you both back to bed."

Adam reluctantly obeyed, and Teresa tucked them both in snuggly as the thunder came again, though not nearly as loud this time, and he ducked under his covers.

"Try to go back to sleep," Teresa whispered. "I'm going downstairs to make sure everything is all right, and then I'll be back up, okay?"

Katie nodded weakly, and the covers over Adam's head bobbed. Teresa left the room and made her way downstairs to make sure whatever she had heard was not something that needed immediate attention. She hoped the worst it could be was that a branch or some other debris from the storm had blown across the yard and maybe broken a window. Or it might just have been some poor, terrified creature from the woods having found its way inside to escape the storm. Though the more she thought about it, neither of those options seemed especially likely. She had not heard breaking glass or what might have been the random scurrying of tiny feet on the hard floors.

What suddenly came into her mind was the possibility that some intruder might have broken in, taking advantage of the storm, as well as knowing she was all alone. What she was sure she had heard earlier was the regular plodding and clomping of heavy footsteps as if someone were searching for something. That possibility chilled her through and through, but still, she went forward. She was the lone wall of defense for her kids regardless of what had happened. But as she reached the lower level and was on her way toward the sounds, Teresa suddenly realized that if this latter situation were at play, she had absolutely no idea what she would use or how she would go about defending herself or Adam and Katie. In the end, none of the possibilities that flashed through her brain ever mattered.

The next morning, the storm had blown itself out and the sun was out doing its best to dry out the soggy ground when Tony Longmore arrived at Aberdeen Estates to assess the situation for any damage. The mansion itself looked fine from the outside, which allowed him to exhale in relief as a few other projects he had going on just now had not escaped so easily. But he furrowed his brow when no one answered the door when he knocked. He called out to Teresa as well but got no answer. He did not like just walking into a client's home unannounced or uninvited, but something did not feel right. When he stepped inside, he found Adam and Katie sitting huddled together under a thick blanket on the stairs, shaking. They appeared utterly terrified and panicked, though they seemed to not even acknowledge his presence even when he spoke their names.

Tony got one of his guys to sit with them after he finally got Katie to look at him and talk. But she was still miles away, psychologically, only saying "the parlor" over and over like some chant. Tony had no idea what was going on, but for these normally outgoing and bubbly kids to be so shut down, he was pretty sure whatever was in the parlor was going to be very bad news. He and his worker exchanged a nervous look between them, and Tony went to the room that Katie had indicated. He stopped at the doorway and just stared. Just inside the room was the very dead body of Teresa Thompson, a pool of congealing blood under her head. Without taking another step, he pulled out his phone and called 9-1-1.

The police were summoned, and an emergency call was made to Jonathan in Chicago to come home immediately as there had been an accident. By the time Jonathan got back to Green Pond, a thorough investigation was underway, and Tony and his wife did their best to comfort the absolutely distraught and nearly hysterical Jonathan Thompson. Tony filled in the detective who was sent while his wife took the kids under her wing to try to keep them from completely falling apart as well. Though small, the Green Pond Police Department did a very professional and complete investigation based on what Tony told them he had found when he had arrived that morning.

Though they normally would look at the husband as their initial suspect, the detective immediately ruled Jonathan out when he showed his proof of having been away on business in Chicago and his alibi was corroborated. Adam and Katie were also eventually questioned by a very kind and compassionate female officer, Sergeant Stephanie Miller, once some time had passed, but all they could tell anyone was that they had found their mother right where the police had found her when she did not come back to bed the night before. The investigation was supported by county and state officials when the local force asked for help, feeling they might not have the necessary experience to make all the right moves. But in the end, no one was ever charged or arrested for Teresa Thompson's murder.

All the police—both local and from outside Green

Pond—agreed that she had indeed been murdered. In fact, she had been stabbed multiple times. But all they had to go on was a dead body and a lot of blood. No murder weapon was ever found, nor was there any other physical evidence uncovered—no prints, no hair fibers except those of the victim, no indication Teresa Thompson had put up any struggle, not even any signs of a forced entry to give them any leads to follow. Rewards were offered for any information to help the police find the murderer, but after a year went by, nothing helped, and the case was filed as unsolved and cold.

MAY 2008

*H*arold and Chloe Reynolds had been trying to have children for what seemed to them to be forever, and the latest go-around had felt as if they had finally succeeded after multiple disappointments and heartache. But when Chloe had to be rushed to the hospital far ahead of her due date, she knew it was not a good sign. She had been down this road too many times not to have just as good an idea of what was likely transpiring as her OB-GYN, who had endured all her anguish and grief as if it were happening to her as well. Chloe felt almost numb this time around, like she was in some morbid remake of the old Bill Murray film, *Groundhog Day*, as they wheeled her inside the hospital. And if she had not come so close this time, she supposed it would have been easier to accept, but acceptance was just out of her reach. Chloe felt as if she were being punished by not being the one thing she had wanted with all her heart since she was very young—a mother.

WALTERBORO, SOUTH CAROLINA
1995

$\mathcal{C}$hloe Reynolds—Chloe Peters, back in Walterboro, South Carolina—had grown up in a loving and close family surrounded by many siblings. She could not have asked for better parents, she supposed, once she got into the world and heard some of the horror stories from classmates and co-workers about what they had endured growing up with severely dysfunctional parents. Her childhood was not perfect, but then again, whose was? But looking back as she headed off to college and then went into the work-place, it seemed a magical and idyllic time in her life. Chloe had observed her parents over the years and stored away what she had experienced through them for future use when she was a parent. She went away to The College of Charleston following high school with no real idea of what she wanted to do with her life other than to be a mom.

But as she drifted into her sophomore year, she began to focus her interests and study on education, knowing she wanted to work with children as well as have her own someday. It was perhaps not as ambitious a goal as many of her friends on campus, but Chloe knew what she wanted and never felt like she might be missing something by never wavering from her childhood dreams. Her college days were unremarkable relative to most others, but when she graduated, she was rewarded with an opportunity to help shape a new elementary-level education program for an experimental school system the governor had launched as part of his campaign platform. It was not solely public nor private, and the challenge was just what Chloe knew was a perfect fit for her. The keystone location was over in Hampton, and Chloe was thrilled the new opportunity would allow her to stay close to her large family.

HAMPTON, SOUTH CAROLINA 1997

*M*eanwhile, over in Hampton, South Carolina, Harold Reynolds experienced a much different life growing up. That was not to say that he had the dysfunctional family life that had horrified Chloe, but relative to the large and warm environment she had thrived in, Harold was an only child born to parents who did the best they could for him with the limited resources available. Tom and Helen Reynolds were not exactly poor, but they also were not quite middle-class, either. Harold had never felt that he went without anything, but deep down, he knew his folks struggled to keep their heads above water and that many sacrifices were being made to try to make his life easier and more comfortable than either one of them had experienced.

Early on, Harold found he had a real talent and love for creating things out of scraps he might encounter when scavenging as the adventurous child he was. That ability soon morphed into a more sophisticated and refined one in the field of carpentry, especially detailed woodworking and refinishing old, abandoned pieces to make them appealing to people furnishing old, period-era homes in South Carolina. Unlike Chloe, who had discovered her calling once she was enrolled in college, Harold had known that life was for him instantly.

His folks were a bit disappointed when he announced he had no desire to continue his education beyond high school. However, they were not horribly shocked, seeing as how he was always tinkering with some woodworking project in the small shed his father kept out back. Harold certainly could have gone off to school had he chosen that route. His grades were good enough, and he understood complex concepts and ideas much quicker than most of his classmates. But he just did not have any interest. He wanted to be a builder, and he knew getting his hands dirty with an experienced mentor was the only way to achieve his dreams. And so he did.

HAROLD SIGNED on with who he considered a true woodworking artisan soon after he graduated from high school, and that was, as far as he was concerned, when his real education began. Michael Dewer was well-known throughout Hampton, and Harold considered himself very fortunate that Mr. Dewer had offered him the chance to come on board as his apprentice/assistant. Dewer was not known to take on young partners, and Harold did everything possible to ensure his new boss did not regret breaking his hard and fast rule. Within a year or so, both of them were thrilled about the arrangement, and Harold looked forward to getting more and more independence from Dewer as his own skillset was honed and refined.

But he had not expected the opportunity to come as quickly as it had. Harold went into work one day, but he could not find Dewer anywhere. It was only after a long search that he found his boss collapsed inside the storage shed they used to keep some of the more precious lumber protected from the weather. He rushed to Dewer's side as panic rose in his chest. His elder mentor was still alive, but his breathing was labored and thready. Harold called for an ambulance immediately and followed in his car as they rushed Dewer to the emergency room. Harold waited patiently as he paced the waiting room to get word of his boss's condition. But when a very fatigued and wrung-out doctor in surgery scrubs approached him, Harold knew it was not good news.

DEWER'S FAMILY summoned Harold to a lawyer's office following the memorial service though he had no idea why. He was just a partner/employee, and being included in this meeting—for a reading of Dewer's will —felt uncomfortable as he was still trying to deal with the loss of his beloved mentor and wondering what in the hell he would do with his life now. Harold sat quietly as the lawyer, Frederick Davenport, went through all the introductions and formalities as Dewer's assets and estate were parceled out to various family members. He still had no idea why he was there, but in the next five minutes, it became crystal clear. Dewer's wife, Marjorie, took Harold's hand in hers and nodded to Davenport to continue.

Harold sat slack-jawed as Davenport read from the will that indicated that Dewer had left him his business, including his clientele. He knew Dewer had loved his work but never in his wildest imagination had he expected this. When Davenport finished all the legalese and looked to smile, Harold just looked over at Marjorie Dewer and gaped.

"I…I…Mrs. Dewer," Harold stammered, "is this for real?"

She smiled and chuckled. "That it is, my boy. Michael spent a lifetime building his business, and as his health began to falter lately, he was terrified it would just evaporate and fade away to nothing since we have no children to pass it on to."

"But…I'm hardly family, ma'am. Certainly, there must be someone else."

"As far as Michael was concerned, you were, Harold. There was hardly an evening he didn't come home without extolling the virtues of this extraordinary young apprentice he had found."

Harold blushed. Their relationship had been cordial enough, but the praise was new to him. "I don't know what to say, ma'am…except thank you and trust that I will continue his business in the manner I know he would approve of."

"I know you will, Harold. Otherwise, Michael would never have handed you the keys, so to speak. He never said as much, but I have this gut feeling you were the son he never had."

Harold bowed his head as his eyes filled with tears.

7

HAMPTON, SOUTH CAROLINA 2005

*A*fter a few days, Harold was finally getting used to the idea that the business was now his to run, though he certainly had no idea how to really go about that. Everything he had learned from Michael Dewer had been surrounding technical skills for his craft. Fortunately, though, Madeline Emery, the long-term, part-time clerk Michael had employed for as long as Harold could remember, was more than willing to stay on and help ease him into what was going to be required to keep the business humming on all levels. Come to find out, it was actually Madeline who dealt with most of the business issues not related to the hands-on carpentry and other construction aspects. For that, Harold was incredibly grateful.

Time went by, and though he would never forget his mentor and old boss, Harold soon found himself on top of things as if Michael were still around. In fact, things were growing beyond anything Michael had ever envisioned...or even desired, Harold thought. Dewer had been, it seemed to him, content to just have his small operation remain where it was size-wise with no real interest in growing it any larger. But Harold was young, and he and Madeline saw that if they did not expand, they could very well just become obsolete one day. With a combination of utilizing Michael Dewer's name and reputation, Harold's own skills, and Madeline's keen insight for ideas on generating new business, Dewer Carpentry and Building became Dewer Carpentry and Construction Associates as they took on several new and promising workers, just as Dewer had with Harold.

Within months, their gamble had paid off, and if Michael Dewer had come walking in the door by then, he probably would not have recognized his old company. It was certainly not some huge mega entity by any means, but they were expanding—slowly and carefully under Madeline's eagle eye—and new clients were coming to them quicker than ever. Harold's new hires learned the ropes way faster than he had, and soon, he was able to let them have a free hand when he assigned new projects. He still had the final say when the projects came in, but once all looked good, he was able to allow his new employees to run the show without him having to physically be on every job site... though he still dropped by from time to time to make sure the quality he demanded was being met.

And it was that freedom of his responsibilities that eventually led Harold Reynolds to a path that even a few months earlier he never would have imagined: meeting his soon-to-be wife, Chloe Peters. With the expansion of the business, Harold was often deflecting clients as he simply did not have the hands to take on every project that came through their doors. Over time, he had established relationships with other providers so both entities could shuttle clients back and forth depending on their respective workloads and specifics requested based on each company's strengths. From the outside, Harold supposed that might sound like it was sabotaging his own self-interests, but somehow it all worked out perfectly for everyone.

But when this attractive and energetic young woman waltzed through their doors one day, requesting a project for this new innovative school over in Walterboro, Harold knew it was an account he would not farm out. He and Madeline had heard of this new government-funded initiative, and now that the initial location for the system had just walked into their offices, there was no way he was going to turn it down. It was just too big an opportunity, and it certainly would lead to other sites if all went well. Plus, there was just something about this woman that he was instantly mesmerized with.

Well, to cut to the chase, Harold took on Chloe's school project, which was a roaring success, and Harold was soon awarded the contract for all the follow-up sites as well. Oh…and by the way, as you may have guessed by now, the working relationship between Harold and Chloe grew into something much more personal. A little over a year after she had walked through his doors, Chloe Peters became Chloe Reynolds, and she saw all her dreams from her childhood finally coming true.

8

MAY 2008

*H*arold sat with a disconsolate and deeply depressed Chloe in her room as they both tried to recover from this latest tragedy of a still-born child. Even through all the other failed pregnancies, Chloe had never felt as completely broken and devastated in her life as she did now. Harold had been by her side throughout all the other dark times, doing what he could, but this time, even digging as deep inside himself as he could, Harold felt inadequate to offer consolation and comfort. And as if that crushing blow was not enough, Chloe's OB-GYN sadly informed her that due to all the physical trauma she had endured over the years of her various pregnancies, she would now be unable to ever have a baby at all.

Harold felt like he had absorbed a massive punch to his gut when the news was delivered and he saw what little light and life that Chloe still hung onto seem to flicker and then go out. She just stared straight ahead as if looking at some faraway sight only she could see, not speaking, not crying…nothing…just this near-cata-tonic trance had come over her, and he felt completely impotent.

* * *

AFTER SOME TIME back home to recover physically and emotionally, Chloe seemed just as empty and depressed as she had when she had lost the child. With grave concerns that he might lose her forever into whatever black hole she had fallen, Harold suggested it might be time for Chloe to consult a therapist who had some professional expertise in helping people over experiences of extreme grief and loss such as hers. After some initial reluctance, Chloe agreed to give it a try, figuring nothing would make her circumstances any worse. Chloe engaged the services of Dr. Cynthia Abrams, and to her surprise and amazement, she was, after a series of meetings with her, beginning to feel better than she had since the incident. Harold held his rhetorical breath while he watched the slow but progressive changes in Chloe as she began to emerge from her depression and begin to resemble who she once had been with him.

Once she seemed to be well on her way back to normal, Dr. Abrams summoned them both to her office for a joint session and to offer a suggestion that she had often seen have miraculous effects in getting similar patients over the last hump they were facing.

"Chloe," Dr. Abrams began, "likely, you will never be completely free of this horrible memory, but I have found with other patients who have gone through severe trauma that a temporary hiatus from the site of that trauma can work wonders."

Chloe and Harold said nothing.

"It doesn't have to be anywhere far away or even for a very long time, but it has been my experience that just the physical separation can make the adjustment for the rest of your life much more effective. This is not something you should ever expect to just one day magically vanish from your memory, nor should you try to force that."

It was blunt and direct, but that was one thing Chloe had liked about Dr. Abrams from the beginning...she was compassionate and no-nonsense all at the same time. They talked about this suggestion between the three of them a bit longer, and Chloe agreed with her therapist. Her innate love of children would never die, and maybe an opportunity to work closely with kids might as well be beneficial in her recovery and sidestep a major breakdown down the road.

"Plus," Cynthia added, "just staying busy and distracted from everything that reminds you of Hampton for a while will keep your brain occupied and keep you from constantly obsessing over your loss."

9

MAY 2008

*B*oth Harold and Chloe were undecided about Dr. Abrams's proposal, but once they got home and talked it over, it began to make more and more sense. Chloe had been making continuous progress forward under Cynthia's care, so seeing as how she was the expert, they decided to follow her counsel. Deep down, Harold was gratefully relieved at having a real action plan to follow as he still felt pretty ineffective at offering any significant help to Chloe other than just basic comfort and reassurance. The only sticking point from Chloe's perspective was regarding Harold's business and how he would continue to manage that remotely if they left Hampton for some undetermined period.

Harold told her not to worry about that, and he set off for the office to gather his staff to lay out how they would continue to operate based on this unexpected development. Madeline and his employees all sat quietly as he went through what Dr. Abrams had proposed was best for Chloe's continued recovery. Though not exactly family, they were all well aware of what had happened and made sure Harold knew they had his back no matter what. They had a full plate at the moment, so taking on new business, though never considered, was not such a priority, and Harold had full confidence in his guys to keep the technical portion of everything on track. But the look in Madeline's eyes made him know he would have to talk with her a bit more.

"Okay, Madeline," Harold said once the guys had gone off to their respective job sites, "let's hear it."

She pursed her lips and exhaled slightly. "Harold, you know I would do anything for you, right? But I'm just a little hesitant not to have you here, overseeing the management."

"Look, Madeline, at this point, it is really you who runs this office anyway, for the most part. The guys are more than capable, and we don't envision this time away being too long. I have full confidence in you, and if anything really crazy goes down, then I'll just be a phone call away."

She blushed slightly at his praise and nodded. "Thanks, Harold. I'll do my best."

"I know you will, Madeline. And when I get back, I think it's time to discuss making you more than what your role has been so far if you are interested."

She arched her eyebrows.

"I would really like to have you here as a real partner moving forward. If it appeals to you, I would like you to be a joint owner with me. I really can't run this place without you."

"Gosh, Harold," she replied in an uncharacteristically subdued tone, "I don't know what to say."

"Just think it over and see how it feels on your own here while I'm away, and we can talk when I get back."

She smiled and hugged him warmly before he took off to go home for the day so he and Chloe could figure out just where they might go. As he walked to his car, Harold smiled broadly, sure that Madeline's vital skills for the business had just been locked in for good.

OVER THE NEXT FEW DAYS, Harold and Chloe considered several options to put Cynthia's plan into action, but nothing they looked at seemed right. Harold was actually searching for something that would allow Chloe to interact with children on some level while maybe finding some side work for himself just to make their routines away as normal as possible. As well, he had never been idle, going all the way back to when he had been in high school and had begun his chosen career. He figured it would be good for his mental health to stay busy and keep his skills honed, especially if some need to get back to Hampton in an emergency arose.

And oddly enough, it was a chance and casual conversation with a guy he had done work for years ago, when Michael Dewer was still alive, that made it all come together. Back when he had just signed on with Michael, they had taken on a project with Joseph Bankston to redo an old house from this large single-family home into a B&B operation. Harold had unexpectedly bumped into Joseph on a trip to town to drop off some paperwork with the city for permits on another project, and they took a break to have coffee at a small café in town.

Joseph had remembered Harold well from the work he had done for him earlier and was thrilled at how successful he had been at turning the Dewer enterprise into something his old boss would have certainly approved of. Harold filled him in on all that had happened as they both caught up with one another before mentioning what he and Chloe had gone through and what they were trying to find now to continue her recovery. Joseph got this odd and faraway look in his eyes as he just nodded and sipped at his coffee before a smile came over his face.

"You know, Harold," he offered after a pause, "I might just have exactly what you're looking for."

"You're kidding?" Harold replied, taken back a bit.

"Nope. I know of this guy over in Green Pond who has been looking for some help on an old mansion he's renovating. You ever been there?"

"Nope...I know of it but have never been."

"Anyway, he lost his wife and needs some expertise like yours to work with his general contractor. And to top it off, he's looking for a nanny/teacher to take care of his kids because he travels quite a lot for work."

Harold sat silent and dumbfounded as he listened to Joseph's spiel. It seemed impossibly perfect. He asked a few more questions, and after giving him as many details as he knew, Joseph handed him the man's name and phone number. Harold looked at the card with Jonathan Thompson's information.

"I'll give him a ring this afternoon and give him a heads up about you if you want me to."

"That would be great, Joseph. Thanks so much!"

Harold rushed home to run this all by Chloe before making any calls to this Jonathan Thompson to see what she thought first. Just as he had when Bankston had sprung the opportunity on him, Chloe sat, her mouth agape, taking in the seemingly ideal nature of it all. Harold just ran the rough ideas by her.

"Widower?" Chloe asked.

"Apparently so...Joseph didn't give me any real details, just that he had lost his wife a few years back, and the progress on the mansion got put on hold following her death."

"Anything on the kids? Ages, boys or girls... anything like that?"

"I don't know, but he needs someone like you to homeschool them as well as just take care of them in general, so I would assume they are fairly young. If it sounds good, I can find out more when I talk to him later."

Chloe nodded. "Is it just me, Harold, or does this seem absolutely perfect for us?"

"Nope...not just you."

Harold let those words pass by without further comment, but in the back of his mind, a little voice crept up with the message his mom had often said, "If it's too good to be true, then most times it is…."

Harold knew she was right, but then again, they needed this opportunity soon, and he would not know for sure if it was actually going to work out until they met Thompson and got a better idea of the whole arrangement. In his experience, he never took on any new opportunity without getting a sense of personalities, though this would have to present some real red warning flags to make him not look into it deeper. Harold could see that Chloe was really interested, and the move was, after all, primarily for her. It would be a step back for Harold to be working for someone else, but then again, it was just temporary, and there was always the chance that he might pick up some new techniques or skills he had yet to learn.

10

MAY 2008

Harold called Thompson later that afternoon, ensuring that Bankston had called ahead to make him aware that he would be reaching out. Though sounding a bit cold and all business on the phone, Thompson assured him that he had and that Bankston had been very complimentary regarding Harold's work. He reiterated that his contractor needed some skilled assistance because there was a labor shortage in Green Pond at the moment, as well as help with his kids when he traveled since his current nanny had recently left.

Harold described Chloe's background in education there in Hampton and her deep love of working with children. Thompson did not comment but just offered them a live interview to see the place and see if this was going to be a good fit for everyone involved. As an added bonus, Thompson had said, they would be set up to stay at the mansion while the work went on since Chloe would need to be with the children around the clock. Harold thanked him and told him they could meet with him later in the week. They arranged a good time for all three of them, and Harold sat down with Chloe to fill her in.

"What do you think, Harold?"

"Well…on the phone, Thompson seemed a bit gruff and rough around the edges, but otherwise, I can't see any reason not to at least go over to meet with him."

"Gruff? Does that mean he might be difficult to deal with?"

Harold shrugged. "Hard to say. Maybe I'm being a bit too harsh. His demeanor just came across as all business. And I understand he is still mourning the loss of his wife so that might be a factor at play as well. Anyway, I have dealt with various personalities over the years in the business world so that doesn't really concern me. This gig is primarily for you, Chloe. I'm sure we'll have a much better idea of the fit after seeing everything in person and meeting the people involved. Sound good?"

Chloe nodded and smiled, deeply touched that Harold was putting her well-being and mental health at the top of the priority list for them. She knew this hiatus from his business was not ideal, and it made her extremely grateful she had a husband who was making such a sacrifice without question or concern for his own situation. Harold left Chloe at the house while he went to the office to tell Madeline what had been set up for the upcoming interview and that he would be out that day.

It felt odd to Harold to possibly be preparing to

hand over the reins to Madeline, even temporarily, despite his utmost trust and confidence in her to run the show in his absence. He had not just been blowing smoke when he had told her she was actually running the office anyway, but still, it felt odd. Ever since Michael had died, Harold had been at the helm, even if Madeline had been more than just an employee to him while he scaled the steep learning curve of being in charge and making all the final decisions.

He smiled to himself as he thought back on all the times she had caught him just before he had made a serious blunder or two and gotten him back on track. And unless there was something blatantly obvious during the upcoming interview that made them turn it down, Madeline was indeed going to be in charge. They sat together for a few minutes so Madeline could make sure she fully understood everything that would fall to her if Harold and Chloe took this offer and had to leave quickly. He suppressed a grin as he patiently let her run through a litany of concerns that he knew she already was doing as part of her job anyway.

"You will be fine, Madeline," Harold finally said when she paused. "You are already doing all of this anyway, right?"

She reddened a bit and smiled, nodding. "Yeah...I suppose I am. But you've always been here. This will be very different for me."

"Besides," Harold replied, "we haven't even accepted an offer yet."

"Just getting ready, I guess," Madeline said. "It seems like a perfect situation."

"That it does. But let's just take this one step at a time. We will talk again after the interview if we do decide to sign on. Okay?"

Madeline nodded.

* * *

HAROLD RETURNED HOME to find Chloe immersed in various open files on her laptop as she sat at the dining room table with a glass of wine at her elbow. He walked over and kissed her on the top of the head as he peered over her shoulder.

"What's all this, Chloe?"

"Oh…just curious about Green Pond. It's one of those small places you might blow right past on a drive and not even give it a second glance. I just thought I should try to see what I could find out about it before it became a temporary home for us."

Harold laughed out loud.

"I say something funny, pal?" she asked with a grin.

"No, not really. It's just we haven't even seen the place nor talked to this Jonathan Thompson in person, and everyone just assumes it's a done deal. I'm not sure who's more convinced of that at this point, you or Madeline."

Chloe chuckled as well. "You having second thoughts? I mean…, it has to be tough handing over control of the company to her, right?"

"Not at all. Madeline is more than capable. And Green Pond is just a stone's throw from Hampton if I'm truly needed in person. But no…this seems pretty ideal for us, and it would take a major hurdle blocking us for me to say no."

"Good….because it feels right to me already, and this little town is really cute."

Harold got his own glass of wine, and after a brief call to Joseph Bankston to thank him for the introduction, he and Chloe retired to the back deck to watch the sunset and dream of this new adventure that lay ahead of them.

11

MAY 2008

*H*arold and Chloe took off early Friday morning for Green Pond so they could arrive well before the scheduled interview and get a feel for and look around the town itself. As Chloe had mentioned back at the house when Harold had found her looking over what information she could find about Green Pond—and with the small size of it that was scant—it really was the kind of place one might just breeze through without even slowing down. But Harold had to agree with Chloe that the small village had its charm and allure. There was really just one main thoroughfare with a few side streets that branched off here and there for locals' homes.

The street was pretty empty, except for a few people milling about, running errands, or standing in groups of two or three engaged in conversations. As far as they could see, there was not really much to speak of in the way of commerce once you saw the general store, a post office, a small hardware store, and a little combination medical clinic housing a GP, a dentist, and an optometrist. It was a quiet and welcome relief from the activity in Hampton, though even Hampton was not exactly a beehive of scurrying people on any given day. They eased down the road, glancing about as they went, and Chloe pointed out spots that looked interesting for them to take a closer look at if this whole situation did, in fact, pan out and they ended up living here for a bit.

Harold could not ignore some odd stares and even a weird vibe they were getting from several of the people on the street that they said hello to, but they were new in town, and he figured it was just that and nothing more. The directions that Thompson had given them had seemed clear enough over the phone, but now that they were there, the landmarks and other spots he had mentioned to guide them out to the mansion were not so evident. But one not-so-stand-offish man at the edge of town gave them better directions, and they were soon on their way out to Aberdeen Estates to talk with Jonathan Thompson. Harold thanked the guy and shook his head when he realized that without his assistance, they would have been hopelessly lost...even though that seemed ludicrous in such a small locale. He hoped Thompson would prove to be a better employer than he was a travel guide.

They left the paved road of the town and drove over a series of hard-packed but unrutted dirt roads just south of town until a worn and weathered wooden sign just outside a gravel drive indicated they had arrived. Harold turned into the drive and crept slowly up the gravel path, negotiating the various piles of materials, tools, and supplies here and there that let him know there was indeed an active construction site in progress. They slowed to a stop as they neared the mansion itself, and a middle-aged man appeared and waved…Thompson, Harold assumed. They both returned his greeting and walked over to shake his hand.

"Mr. and Mrs. Reynolds, I assume?" the man asked.

"That's us. I'm Harold, and this is my wife, Chloe. You're Mr. Thompson?"

"I am…Jonathan is fine. Sorry for the mess, but it's an obvious sign as to just how badly I need some help here. My contractor has his hands full and is a bit over-whelmed at the moment, I'm afraid."

Harold smiled and nodded. It was no big deal to him. He had seen much worse back in Hampton. Thompson seemed nice enough, but just like on the phone, his tone and demeanor felt a touch cold and stiff, even as he tried to apologize for the chaotic condition of grounds. He was unsure if this was the man's normal personality or it was still being colored to some degree by ongoing mourning over the loss of his wife. Harold knew for a fact that if he had to endure the loss of Chloe, either as suddenly and as unexpectedly as Thompson had his wife, or otherwise, that he would likely feel a debilitating sorrow he could not even begin to imagine.

With that in mind, he and Chloe followed Thompson over to a small outdoor sitting area just to the side of the front entrance for the "formal" interview. They sat and politely accepted tall glasses of iced tea from their potential employer as the warm sun of the early afternoon bore down on them.

"Why don't I go through what I'm looking for in detail," Jonathan said as he set aside his drink.

Harold nodded.

"Basically, I want to get this renovation back on track...or at least as close to where it was as possible just recently. Tony Longmore, my contractor, is the best, but there's only so much he can do with the trouble we're having getting him good, dependable help. That's number one."

He paused to take a sip.

"As well, I need someone experienced with child-care, and if possible, to tutor since the nanny I had left unexpectedly. I wasn't expecting to find the solution to my situation with one shot, but after talking to both Joseph Bankston and then you, I'm hopeful this might happen."

"As to your needs for renovation help, Jonathan," Harold began, "I'll have a better idea of whether or not my contributions might be a good fit, but at least for now, this seems like a good fit for me."

"Good...I'm familiar with your work, Harold. I researched your company and what you did to build it into what it is now following the founder's death. Your skill and expertise are impressive. My only concern is how it's going to feel for you to not be in charge of a project based on what you normally do over in Hampton."

Harold nodded his understanding. "I appreciate the

compliment, Jonathan. And as to your concern…well… we're looking into this opportunity for a break from a recent family issue we had back in Hampton. We both just need a short time away from everything there, and working alongside Tony will be no problem, I assure you."

Chloe glanced at Harold as he relayed that bit of information, wondering if he would divulge more. Her stomach was in turmoil, hoping he did not and that Thompson would not ask for any more details. She was not keen on having some stranger privy to their personal lives. But Harold had no intention of saying anything more. He just felt he needed to preface their situation to make Thompson understand that being second banana here would not be a problem. He would never have revealed any more details out of consideration for Chloe. Thankfully, Thompson did not probe further, and Chloe sighed with relief as he just nodded.

"Fair enough," Jonathan replied. "Now as to the children," he continued as he looked over at Chloe. "My kids have been through a nightmare, as you might imagine, with the loss of their mother. And having the last nanny up and leave with no notice or warning was a major setback for both of them after they had just begun to recover. I need to know that even on the temporary basis that you might take care of them, that you can provide the stability and dedication to them that they need."

"Of course," Chloe replied.

"There's a chef on staff, so there's no reason to worry about meals, but otherwise, I need you to see to their daily needs as well as pick up their home-schooling where the last nanny left off. The public schools here aren't bad, but emotionally, I don't think they're quite ready to be thrown back into that challenge, if you get my meaning."

"I do, Jonathan," she replied. "What are their names and their ages?"

"I have a son, Adam, who just turned eight, and a daughter, Katie, who is almost nine. They were both outgoing and extroverted before their mother died, but as you might expect, that has changed considerably. But they are both very bright and just need the right person to help them heal."

Chloe nodded as she tried to imagine how painful and awful it must be for them both to have gone through this. Upon his follow-up inquiry about her qualifications, Chloe carefully and methodically filled him in on her upbringing in a large family, her background in education from college, and her current position with the new school system in Hampton at which she had taken an extended sabbatical. Thompson nodded along, and both Harold and Chloe could see he was impressed and satisfied.

"Well," Thompson said after a brief pause, "you both seem perfect. Any other questions that I can answer concerning the opportunity?"

MAY 2008

$\mathcal{H}$arold hesitated a beat before saying anything. The man had obviously been through the wringer, and the last thing he needed was to relive the trauma. But thinking back to what his mother had said about "things looking too good to be true," he decided to go ahead and ask.

"Actually, Jonathan," Harold said at last, "if it is not too personal or painful, I was wondering if we could find out just why—and pardon my bluntness here—everything went so badly here?"

Once the words were out of his mouth, Harold was afraid he might have stepped over a line, but he did not want to get the two of them in the middle of something they would regret later. Thompson exhaled deeply, set his drink aside, and looked away at the towering trees to the east as the ice cubes in his glass clinked to the bottom.

He was not especially keen on having to air it out to strangers, but in the end, Thompson did not want the real story of what had happened here to get back to them from someone else in Green Pond. The small-town gossip-wire was an inevitable reality. Plus, if any of the details of what had happened to Teresa were going to make them uncomfortable, too uneasy to do what he wanted to hire them for, he needed to know now. Once he was away for travel would not be the time to find that out.

"I suppose turnabout is fair play since I asked about you two, Harold. Okay...here's what happened."

Harold sat back, relieved that Thompson had not taken offense at what he had asked and that his curiosity had not nixed their candidacy. Jonathan took him back to the days when he and Teresa had arrived here in Green Pond from New York City and why he had walked away from his successful and thriving career.

"Mostly," Jonathan went on, "I had just lost my motivation to keep doing what I had been doing for many years. Maybe I was just experiencing burnout or something. Anyway, that combined with our concern over what Adam and Katie might get exposed to in the city as they grew sealed the deal. I pulled the plug, and we came here for a better quality of life, I suppose."

"Just a relaxing step back living in the rural coun-tryside?" Chloe asked with a smile.

Thompson nodded but did not return her smile, keeping the same neutral and hardened expression on his face that they had seen since they had arrived.

"But after a while, I discovered that my...hell I can admit it...my type-A personality was just not cut out for what I had planned. I was going a little stir-crazy, I guess, with nothing to keep my brain occupied like it had all my professional life."

"Not much of a golfer or fisherman, eh?" Harold interjected with a grin.

Thompson did not exactly grin back, but there was a tinge there that Harold saw hiding behind his façade trying to peek through.

"Yeah…I never really was a 'hobby kind of guy.' I just had my career and my family. So to try to keep sane, I called around to some of my former colleagues and did some research in preparation for launching a new business."

Harold was a little more than mildly curious as to what that new venture was exactly, but he did not probe, figuring he had been fortunate up to this point getting Thompson to open up at all.

"Which led to a lot of travel away from Green Pond?" Chloe asked.

Jonathan sighed deeply, and they both saw his eyes fill with tears. He wiped them away and went on after a brief hesitation. "Unfortunately, yes," Thompson replied with a tinge of deep regret in his voice. "At the time, there was no other option if I were to make this new thing a reality, but if I could take it all back, I would."

"Oh?" Harold asked.

"Absolutely. Being away left Teresa on her own a lot. After much debate, she assured me she would be fine. That Green Pond was no New York City, and all that. But if I had not been so self-centered and ego-driven, she might still be alive."

"Oh no…" Chloe said as her hand went to her mouth.

Jonathan nodded as he relayed that she had been murdered while he was away on an out-of-town trip to round up investors for the new business. No one said anything for a few minutes as Harold and Chloe sat stunned by this revelation, both truly regretting they had pried this out and were making him relive it again.

"I'm really sorry, Jonathan," Harold finally said. "I had no idea. You don't need to go through all that again."

Thompson waved him off. "Green Pond is a really small place, Harold. If I hadn't told you, you would have found out soon enough, I imagine."

"Did they find the killer?" Harold asked.

"Nope. The police were very thorough, but they never found anything to help them identify a plausible suspect. Local, county, and state cops were all over the case, but in the end…nothing."

"How horrible!" Chloe exclaimed as she felt a tear come to her own eye.

"Anyway…after that, I just lost my urgency to finish the mansion while I tried to deal with Teresa's murder."

"But you also mentioned a labor shortage?" Harold asked. "That related to the hiatus as well?"

Jonathan gave him a long, hard look and then shrugged. "I might as well give you the skinny on that, too, seeing as how any number of gossipmongers in Green Pond is bound to let you know anyway. Long before we acquired Aberdeen Estates, there was this long-standing…oh…I guess you could call it a local legend or folklore that the mansion was haunted."

"For real?" Harold asked. "I mean actual ghosts or poltergeists or possession…that kind of thing?"

For the first time, Jonathan grinned. "So some say. I have no patience with any of that and just never looked into the history of the place, but yeah. If you talk to the right people in town, that's the belief of some. And once that kind of ridiculous talk began to filter over to Tony's crew, many of the workers began to claim they had seen or heard odd things, especially near sunset, to make them believers as well."

"And they quit, vowing never to come back?" Harold asked.

"Yep…and once that happened, it was near impossible to get anyone new from town to replace them. Thus the project slowed to a near stop."

"This was before Teresa's murder?" Chloe asked.

"It was. So with my wife's murder on top of the haunting legend, plus my depression and grieving, it soon became a mess."

"You mentioned your nanny just left with no notice as well? If you don't mind me asking…that related to all of this?" Chloe asked.

"So I was told. She never came to me face to face, but from others, I heard she was convinced the place was haunted as well as was fearful for her life."

"And you've never seen or heard anything that would make you even suspicious about that kind of thing?" Harold asked.

Jonathan smirked. "Not at all. First of all, I don't believe in such nonsense, but no, I have never experienced anything that would make me wonder. I think Tony and I are the only ones here immune to such ridiculous notions."

Harold said nothing as he glanced sideways at Chloe, knowing she had a vastly different opinion on the subject. But neither commented on this since Jonathan had been very open with them about it all.

13

MAY 2008

"Anything else I can tell you?" Jonathan asked.

Harold and Chloe both shook their heads.

"I think you have been more than forthcoming about the situation, Jonathan. We appreciate your honesty and taking the time to drag yourself through what has been a horrific time in your life."

"So anything about the place giving you second thoughts about my offer? Murder? Ghosts?"

Harold smiled thinly as he looked at Chloe briefly. Without any discussion, he knew she was fine with it all. "Not at all, Jonathan. And we can stay here while I help out Tony and Chloe sees to Adam and Katie?"

"Absolutely. I'm sure Tony would appreciate having someone with your background and expertise around when he's gone, and to try to get the kids back on track, Chloe would obviously need to be here around the clock. But before we seal the deal, I'll find Tony, and you two can meet and talk over what needs to be done moving forward to finish this place and let Chloe meet Adam and Katie so she can at least introduce herself to them. Just to make sure there's not any obvious friction or other problems between anyone... that reasonable?"

"Sounds good," Harold replied.

"As well, I can have Tony give the two of you the ten-cent tour just so you can get a rough orientation. Obviously, it's a pretty big place, and it will take some time to know your way around, but at least he can get you started. He knows the house way better than I do... since all the renovations anyway."

Harold and Chloe nodded their agreement.

"If all looks good after that, when could you start?" Jonathan asked.

"Well, we would need to go back to Hampton and close up a few odds and ends, but how about this coming Monday?"

"Perfect. If all is still agreeable to everyone, I'll inform the chef that you'll be here for the foreseeable future and then have some cleaners in to make sure we have one of the bedrooms suitable for your stay here."

Jonathan turned them over to Tony Longmore, saying he had some personal business to attend to. They thanked him again for the offer, agreeing that unless something arose during their tour with Tony that would give them a reason to not want the gig, he would assume they would begin on Monday as discussed.

"Chances are you might not see too much of me in the next few weeks anyway," Jonathan added. "I have a pressing series of meetings around the country coming up, and seeing as how I'm sure you will sign up here, I need to confirm all those locations and let everyone know I'll be there as previously arranged."

"Anything else, boss?" Tony asked as Jonathan turned to leave.

"Not that I can think of. Just make sure you show them around and give Chloe a few minutes to meet Adam and Katie before they have to head back to Hampton. If for some reason I get stuck someplace and can't get back when I planned, make sure Joanne gets these guys paid on time."

"Will do. Have a safe journey, and we'll talk to you when you get back."

Jonathan waved to them as he headed out to his car and then drove off toward Green Pond.

"Okay, guys, ready for the grand tour?" Tony asked.

They nodded and then followed him inside. Harold and Chloe looked around and then naturally up as the towering ceiling of the foyer caught them by surprise. The oval entryway fed into a long, wide corridor on the right, which had a number of doorways on either side of it. Tony led them down the hallway, pointing out what each room was being redone into now as well as what they had been in the original design.

"Not too much has been changed from when Jonathan and Teresa acquired the place. Just a few upgrades and minor alterations that came with the change in time and the fact that they didn't see much use for some of the outdated and obsolete intentions. But I think you'll see we've done a pretty good job of keeping as much of the original vision as possible.

Jonathan was adamant about trying to maintain as much of that as we could and still make the house modern and functional."

"Very impressive, Tony," Harold said as he lingered in some of the rooms, running his fingers over the fine details of what had been done. "I can't wait to get to work with you on this. I see a lot of techniques and touches I've read about but not actually had a chance to try out in my business."

"Thanks. Jonathan seems pleased as well, and that's what counts for me."

He then walked them through a large kitchen that Chloe marveled at, unable to believe that this was the kitchen for some residential home and not a professional commercial kitchen at a fine restaurant.

"Pretty amazing, huh?" Tony asked as he watched her gaze around.

"I'll say. Jonathan's chef must feel like he's in heaven here."

"That he does. His name is Reggie Foster. I'm not sure if he'll be in by the time you have to leave today or not, but you'll love him. We all do. He's a wizard with a spatula!"

They all laughed.

"Let's head upstairs and do a quick run-through. You can pick out which bedroom you like best, and I'll have my guys spruce it up over the weekend."

They followed him up the highly polished and gleaming oak staircase to find a double corridor arrangement above with numerous bedrooms branching off from each side before coming back together at the back of the mansion to feed into one of the sunniest and most beautiful solariums Chloe had ever seen. It was like walking into some tropical jungle…only without having to worry that a tarantula or some snake might fall out of the vegetation above. On the way back down the hallway, Harold and Chloe picked out a bedroom at random as they all seemed massive and wonderful

"What do you think?" Tony asked as they began to descend the stairs again.

"Hard to put it into words," Harold replied. "How do you keep from getting lost?"

Tony laughed heartily. "To tell you the truth, I still get turned around from time to time. You'll get the hang of it eventually."

"I'm sure it will be a real showplace when you and your crew finish up, Tony," Chloe added.

"Jonathan fill you both in on how he and Teresa came to own this place…his background and all?"

"He did. And your initial crew got spooked by some talk from town about this place being haunted which made getting a crew to work here tough?"

"Sure enough. It's hard to comprehend in this day and age grown men getting so wigged out over some unsubstantiated talk from old-timers in town, but that is in fact what happened."

"The former nanny, too?" Chloe asked.

"So I heard. I don't like to speak ill of anyone behind their backs, but that girl was kind of shaky to begin with. I mean, taking on the nanny position for those two kids—and trust me, Adam and Katie are great kids—seemed a bit out of her abilities if you ask me. I think she realized it was too much for her, and she just used what she had heard from my guys who quit as an excuse to beat feet."

"Huh..." Chloe uttered. "How about Teresa herself?"

"Extraordinary woman, in my opinion. She didn't seem to bat an eye when Jonathan announced his intentions over this new business that would require him to travel extensively and leave her to run the house on her own. My guys and I did what we could for her in his long absences, but for the most part, she never asked much of us, and I never heard her complain...ever."

"Any idea who might have killed her?" Harold asked. "I mean, I know they never found anyone to charge with the murder and all, but from what you say, I find it hard to believe that anyone would wish her ill."

"I couldn't agree more. I can't figure it out unless it was just some random vagrant or something passing through that went nuts on her. I have no idea who would want that sweet, kind woman dead."

"Jonathan still seems to not be over it," Chloe added.

"I think devastated is the adjective you're looking for. He nearly fell apart when he found out. I think it was only that Adam and Katie needed him that he held it together."

"Then could I ask you one more question that Jonathan seemed to disregard as factual?"

"I guess that depends on the question, Harold. I'll answer if I can and don't feel like I'm betraying any confidences that Jonathan had trusted me with."

"Fair enough. He mentioned some stories floating around Green Pond that this place could be haunted. Jonathan said he didn't believe in such nonsense and waved them off as absurd."

Tony howled with laughter. "Oh, that! Phew...I was worried it might be some deep, dark secret about Aberdeen Estates that someone had told you or something."

"Well..." Chloe added, "you've been in Green Pond your whole life, right? You know anything about the place that might warrant such stories?"

"That I have. I'm not quite as strict a skeptic as Jonathan is on the subject, but I can't say I have ever seen or heard anything here that would make me buy into that possibility."

"But is there some old history associated with this place from way back that might have fueled those legends in town?" Harold asked as they sat out front again.

"Well, there's one story I know of. It's one of those things that every kid here in Green Pond hears eventually, usually from some older relative who wants to give them a scare at Halloween."

"Oh?" Chloe asked, her curiosity peaking.

"You believe in this stuff, Chloe?" he asked.

"Let's just say I have an open mind to the possibility."

"Okay, here goes. But let me preface this with the disclaimer that it's just one version of many I know of that make the rounds here from time to time. It's one my grandfather told me when I was about...oh...five or six, I guess. Scared me silly when I first heard it, and ashamed as I am to say so, I passed it along to my kids as well. I have no idea if it has any validity or not if you do believe in such things, but then again, I'm not sure any of these folklore tales really do."

14

MAY 2008

*H*arold and Chloe sat back as Tony began.

"According to my grandfather, Aberdeen Estates was originally constructed in the late 1800s following the reconstruction from the Civil War. As the story goes, Green Pond barely existed back then...more just a kind of crossroads spot than a real town or even a village. Anyway, the man who built it, William Aberdeen, was said to have been a not-so-forthright carpetbagger from somewhere up north. You guys familiar with that term during the reconstructing period here in the South?"

"Opportunists who flooded in to take advantage of many situations during the rebuilding after the war?" Chloe said.

"Very good. Seems Adam and Katie might be getting a great tutor after all."

They all laughed.

"So Aberdeen shows up, and though none of the details are real clear—this is just one place where this story has multiple versions—and this antebellum-style mansion got constructed right here and was named Aberdeen Estates after one of his relatives of some ilk it is said."

"Unethical or illegal funds for the project?" Harold asked.

"Probably. Money was tight in those days, as you can imagine, and none of those guys drifting down here were completely honest. But that's not where the supposed tale of haunting comes from. Well, Aberdeen sets up the mansion for himself and his family...a wife. Penelope and a couple kids. But apparently, Aberdeen was not content to just live in luxury with his family."

"Ah, the plot thickens...." Chloe interjected.

Tony grinned and continued. "He had a taste for the ladies, it seems, and once Penelope found out, it didn't end well. One night, she waited for him as he returned from one of his regular stops at the local tavern after an evening of drinking and one of the local prostitutes. Aberdeen was sure she had no idea of his...uh... extracurricular activities...and never worried about her. But in his impaired state, he fell victim to her as she ambushed him when he walked from the carriage house to the main house, nearly splitting him in half with the ax they used for firewood."

"Holy shit!" Harold exclaimed.

"But even satisfied that she had exacted her revenge on her cheating husband, the guilt in the aftermath was apparently too much for Penelope to bear. She left the ax buried in his eviscerated corpse and hung herself from the high rafters in their barn. The bodies weren't found until a day or so later when the children had not been coming to school."

"Was this ever verified as to actually having happened?" Harold asked with curiosity.

Tony shrugged. "Hard to say, considering the point in time. Most history and records from back then seem to come from being passed down by word of mouth, you know?"

They nodded.

"So to finish the story, it's said that Penelope still haunts the mansion, feeling great remorse for having left her children behind when she impetuously took her own life after dispatching the lecherous William. Over the years, the reports of strange lights and sounds here—and again, I can't say I've ever seen or heard anything—are attributed to Penelope, who is still looking for her children who were sent away to live elsewhere following her suicide."

"Man," Harold exclaimed, "that's one good ripping yarn!"

"It certainly has stood the test of time through all these years, for sure," Tony replied.

Chloe said nothing based on her own at least loose beliefs in such things, wondering if they might get a visit from the poor woman while they were there. It gave her a slight shiver, but she shook it off, doing her best to hide her reaction to the story.

"Well," Tony said after some silence between them, "enough of the dark side of Aberdeen Estates. I know you guys need to get back to Hampton, so how about I drop off Chloe with Adam and Katie so the three of them can get acquainted better while Harold and I roam the grounds and I can show him what's on our to-do list?"

Harold and Chloe nodded as they stood and followed Tony back inside. Chloe went into the bedroom where Adam and Katie were playing quietly at some game between them. Tony and Harold set off to talk about what they would tackle in the coming weeks. Chloe saw immediately that the children were shy and quiet, almost withdrawn in some way, but after what they had been through, she did not see it as that odd. After losing their mother plus having the former nanny just up and bolt with no warning on top of being homeschooled, she figured their slightly stunted social skills were to be expected.

Chloe did her best to try to get the kids to open up a bit and talk to her, but all their replies, though polite and responsive, seemed to be in just single words or short, choppy fragments. Knowing that the children, it seemed, had been the initial ones to discover their mother's body the night she was murdered made Chloe wonder if maybe they knew more than they had let on. Maybe it was out of fear of what they had seen or just the shock of it all and their reticence was a coping mechanism. She was curious but could see that pushing that topic was not wise at the moment. She had just met them and needed a softer touch before considering that conversation.

But as she sat and looked over at them, Chloe could not help recalling what Harold had said about situations being "too good to be true" and wondering if they might have stepped into more than they had bargained for. Now that she knew the horrific tale of William and Penelope Aberdeen on top of what had happened to poor Teresa, she was a bit concerned that being here to heal and recover from her own trauma might be in peril. *How would she heal herself when there seems to be so much darkness in this place already?* It was just giving her a funny feeling…

* * *

AFTER A FEW MINUTES, Tony and Harold reappeared at the bedroom door to collect her. She bid Adam and Katie goodbye, saying she would see them on Monday. They offered up a weak and lukewarm response which made Chloe's heart ache. It was going to take some real effort and patience on her part to win them over after all the losses they had suffered, she knew.

"Ready to go?" Harold asked her.

"I am. You get a good idea of what you and Tony are facing next week?"

"Absolutely. Tony's done a huge amount of work already, but I can definitely see why Jonathan was anxious to get him some help. What is left to do is definitely not a one-man or even a two-man job."

Tony walked them out and waved them along their way as Harold drove back toward Green Pond and the Yemassee Highway and then Route 68 to Hampton.

"You still okay with all of this, Chloe?" Harold asked as they drove.

"Sure…why?"

"I don't know. I mean, the opportunity still seems perfect and all, but the mansion sure seems to have its own unique personality and history, don't you think?"

"No doubt. But with any place that old, there's bound to be at least one story surrounding it that can make you wonder about what went on there in the past and how that might still be. How do I put this without sounding too wonky...I don't know...coloring it?"

"I get you. But even the Aberdeen saga aside—and assuming it's even true based on how Tony framed it— the idea that Teresa Thompson was murdered there doesn't bother you?"

Chloe sighed and looked out her window. "Well...I can't say it doesn't bother me completely, but those kids really need someone, Harold. In just the few minutes I spent with them, I could feel the sadness and anguish lingering over them. Someone needs to step in and try to pull them out of the dark place they've unfortunately fallen into through no fault of their own."

"Okay...just checking. I mean, this whole idea was to help you recover. I just worry that trying to save those kids might impinge on your own healing."

"I thought of that, too, but I think getting my attention and focus on them may be the best therapy for me. Like Dr. Abrams said, getting my mind distracted from my issues may be way more beneficial than any more one-on-one time with her."

"Good enough...but promise me this one thing?"

"Shoot."

"If, at any time, you feel overwhelmed or uncomfortable with our situation in Green Pond, just tell me and we are out of there just like that. No questions asked, no blame placed...okay?"

Chloe nodded and squeezed his hand, once again, eternally grateful she had found Harold Reynolds from among the masses and that he was in her life and always had her back.

15

MAY 2008

*H*arold confirmed with Madeline that they had indeed taken the offer from Jonathan Thompson and were leaving on Sunday afternoon for Green Pond for an indeterminate period. During that absence, he was depending on her to run the business, reiterating that he had the utmost confidence in her. Despite Madeline's uneasy expression from time to time, they went over the last-minute details he thought she might need some repetition on that were not necessarily things she dealt with daily.

"Just remember who is the real brains here, Madeline," Harold said as he stood at the door before leaving. "But I am just a phone call away if anything you can't handle comes up."

Madeline laughed at him and nodded, praying she would not need to interrupt Chloe's last step in her recovery. Harold then headed home to help Chloe pack as they tried to figure out what they would realistically need for what might turn into a longer stay away than they might be anticipating. It was mostly clothes to cover the summer and the early fall if things should require them to be in Green Pond that long, though the difference between summer and early fall in South Carolina was negligible, he thought.

After adding their toiletries to the bag, they both felt ready and headed to bed early, wanting to grab a leisurely breakfast out on Sunday at Chloe's favorite café, "The Broken Yolk," before heading over to Green Pond. Harold figured it would be a nice transition for her rather than just dashing off to the new gig right away. She said nothing but appreciated Harold's approach. She was sure this part of Dr. Abrams's strategy for her was correct, but it still had her a bit nervous. Hopefully, she would not have forced Harold away from his business unnecessarily.

They lingered over eggs and French toast and the wonderful mocha lattes that the eatery was famous for, chatting about all sorts of things but steering clear of anything that had to do with the upcoming plan. They both knew it was going to be quite experimental in nature for both of them. The last thing they wanted to do was obsess over the decision now that it was made and perhaps begin to have doubts. As the clock passed into the afternoon, they finally surrendered their coveted patio table and began the short drive to Green Pond.

"Last chance to say no, Harold," Chloe teased as they left the Hampton town line.

"Too late. Once we have passed the city limits, it's

impossible to turn back. That's not me talking; that's the rule."

She laughed with him and kissed him on the cheek. The sun towered over them in a cloudless sky as they moved down the highway in light traffic as their expectations and outlook for the upcoming challenge were high.

"You sure you're okay with not running the show and just backing up Tony on this deal, Harold?"

"Absolutely. It'll be nice not to have all the decisions and approaches on my shoulders for a change. Plus, Tony can definitely teach me a few things from what I've seen so far…unless this old dog is too far gone."

"Hardly, Harold. If there is one constant with you in your work, it's that you're always looking to learn. He seems like a great guy."

"I couldn't agree more. And according to Tony, there's the outside chance that once the work is over that Jonathan might just put the place on the market."

"Really? After all this work to make it a realization of his vision and design?"

"So he says. He seems to think the place might just hold too many bad memories over what happened to Teresa and his guilt over not having been around to protect her."

"I can see that, but with the violent nature of what happened to his wife, isn't it likely that Jonathan would have been killed as well?"

"Sure, but when things happened as they did, I'm not sure he can see beyond feeling responsible for being out of town."

"That's a tough burden to carry. Maybe divesting himself of the mansion will be the best for everyone. I'm sure it holds a lot of bad memories for the kids as well."

Harold nodded. "How about you? Looked to me like getting through the shells Adam and Katie have built around themselves may take some real effort."

"I'm sure it will. But in my experience, what kids really need is just some consistency and structure. And right now, I think Adam and Katie are running low on both."

"Tony said they were both pretty outgoing and extroverted before, right?"

"That he did. I'm optimistic that with what I can offer them, I can get them on the road back to where they once were. It's going to be a slow road, I'm sure, but just getting them to trust that I will be around and care for them should go a long way to forming a bond of trust to build on."

"I'm glad all I will be doing is building a house. Your job sounds way tougher."

"Everyone has their strengths, Harold. My guess is their isolation following the loss of their mother did not help, either, despite having a nanny to guide them through it."

"And then she up and leaves without a word to anyone."

"Exactly. Time to show these children the love and consistent attention that will bring them back…at least that's my plan."

"I guess Jonathan has tried to do the best he could in the aftermath, too, huh?"

"I'm sure he did, but the man is still suffering as well, Harold. You can see it in his eyes and in the way he carries himself. How can that situation not rub off on the kids, too?"

Harold nodded, recalling how cold and all-business Jonathan had seemed. Chloe was probably right that this was just a reflection of his own ongoing grief.

16

MAY 2008

*H*arold looked up and saw the exit for Green Pond, and they slowed and rolled back into the little town that was to be their home for the next phase of their lives.

"We're back pretty early. Want to look around a bit before we head out to the mansion and get settled in?" Harold asked.

"Yeah, that sounds great."

He parked about halfway down the main street, and they got out and began to stroll the sidewalks. Sunday seemed a quiet day in town, though Harold had an idea that life here never got too busy. They walked along, checking out the major businesses, some of which were shuttered for Sunday, and tried to get a better feel for what was around. They passed an occasional resident who said hello but not much more. When they were doubling back to the car, Harold suggested they take a break and grab an ice cream at a small coffee shop near the car.

"Can I buy you a cone?" he asked.

"Since when did I ever turn down ice cream?"

They got their scoops and ventured out to a small table set up on an outdoor patio just behind the shop itself. They sat under the dense foliage of thick elm trees as a slight breeze fluttered the leaves, giving them a nice break from the sun. Harold thought back to their first impressions of the locals when they had come to interview with Jonathan Thompson, and he decided to run something by Chloe.

"Maybe it is just me, but did you get a weird vibe from any of the people we met on our walk here today?"

"Weird? What do you mean?"

"I don't know...when we were here before, I just picked up on this odd look and feeling from some folks. Today just reminded me of that, but even more so."

"I guess I didn't feel that. Maybe because we are just strangers and new to town?"

"I suppose, but it felt deeper than that to me. Like they didn't want to get too close to us or spend too much time being around us or something. Generally, people in South Carolina are much more open and friendly. I just assumed that a small town like this would be even more so."

"Hmm...this may be way off the mark, but maybe word has gotten around already as to who we are and why we're here. You know, working out at the mansion?"

"Could be. I mean, both Jonathan and Tony have

said the gossip mill here moves faster than the speed of light. Maybe the old legend Tony told us about is more prevalent among the locals than I'd assumed."

"You thinking they feel awkward, knowing we're living and working at a supposed haunted house?"

Harold shrugged. "Just a thought. Who knows? I guess we'll find out as time goes on, huh?"

Chloe nodded. They tossed their napkins and went back outside and drove out to Aberdeen Estates as the sun was beginning its decline toward the western horizon.

17

MAY 2008

*T*ony was just coming around the corner of the mansion when they drove up, and he waved to them.

"Go on up and make yourselves at home in the room you picked put. My guys got it all set up for you. And your timing is great, Chef Foster is here, and dinner is at seven. You never want to miss one of his meals, trust me!"

"Thanks, Tony," Harold shouted back.

Their luggage was pretty minimal considering the situation, and it took only a single trip between the two of them to haul their stuff up the stairs and down to the bedroom. Harold was bringing up the rear when he looked up to see Chloe just standing in the open doorway, staring.

"Something wrong?" Harold asked as he came closer.

"Hardly," Chloe replied. "Look for yourself."

Harold came up to her side, looked into the room,

and saw just what she was talking about. When they had been here just a few days ago, they had seen that the room was on the larger size, but then it had been full of boxes and crates that were being stored while the renovation went on. Now with the room emptied out and cleaned up, it was stunning. Not only was the size a bit overwhelming, but the elegant and opulent décor made them both just stand and gape. It was like walking back in time. Harold was not a big fan of the era of the décor personally, but he had to admit that Jonathan had a keen eye for recreating the period.

"We could always get Tony and his guys to fix up a bigger room if this isn't adequate, Chloe."

"No one likes a smart-ass, Harold. This is…well it's…wow…."

"I think *wow* covers it. I think this is bigger than my first apartment when I took on the apprenticeship with Michael Dewer after graduating from high school. Let's get unpacked. If Tony is right, there's no way I want to miss Chef Foster's dinner."

* * *

HAROLD AND CHLOE found Tony true to his word regarding the food. It was not as fancy as the rooms' décor might indicate, but it was one of the most delicious and filling meals they had ever had. Reggie Foster, the infamous chef, came out to accept their thanks and to introduce himself.

"Glad you liked it. I mainly cater to the kids, but they're not real picky eaters, so if there's anything special you'd like, just let me know in the morning, and if we don't have it, I can always pop by the store to pick up the ingredients."

"Thanks, Chef, but I'm sure we'll be fine with whatever you come up with."

"Fair enough. And it's just plain old Reggie, okay? I just wanted to put that out there in case either of you has any food allergies, or maybe there's something you don't especially care for."

"Tell you what, Reggie," Harold said, "if all the dinners are like this, the only thing I'm going to be allergic to is when we have to go home and cook for ourselves again."

Everyone laughed.

"You're very kind, Harold," Reggie replied when the laughter died down. "And welcome to Aberdeen Estates."

Harold, Chloe, and Tony chatted with Reggie for a few minutes until Chloe could see that Adam and Katie were utterly bored and getting tired.

"I think it is time I began to earn my keep, guys," Chloe said.

She gathered the kids and herded them off to bed, making sure they were comfortable and safe before slipping back out into the hallway to join Harold in their room. He looked up as she came inside and closed their door.

"How did your first interaction go?" he asked.

Chloe shrugged. "Okay, I guess. They still seem pretty unsure and tentative around me, which is understandable, but they got to bed without incident."

"That's a good start, I think. A full day tomorrow should build on that. You'll have those kids eating out of your hands in no time!"

Chloe went to the bathroom to brush her teeth and get ready for bed and found Harold already under the covers. "Tired?" she asked.

"Yeah, a bit. It wasn't such a long day, but I guess the new space and the anticipation of the new situation got to me."

She slid in next to him and began to run her hand along his chest. It wasn't like Chloe never initiated any sexual activity between them, but since they had lost this recent baby, Harold had not been too eager to pursue anything until she was ready. He had been afraid that with the jumble of emotions Chloe had gone through, it would not be wise to do anything but follow her lead. But at the moment, it seemed that she was indeed ready, and he was thrilled she was making the first move. He caressed her breast and felt her respond immediately; as her nipple stiffened, she sighed softly at this touch.

"You sure you're ready?" Harold whispered into her ear as she pulled him closer.

"What do you think?"

They both chuckled, and after a few more precious moments of foreplay, Harold moved on top of her and slowly eased himself inside her. Chloe gasped and dug her fingers into the muscles of his shoulders as they kissed deeply. They knew each other so well that their union was natural and automatic even after the long hiatus. But this time, their lovemaking was slow and

tender and gentle as they began to recapture the inti-
macy of their relationship that had been sidetracked
following the tragedy. Chloe grasped him firmly with
her legs and felt better than she had in months when
her orgasm came to her.

It was not an explosive or jarring thing as had often
been the experience with then when younger but more
of a delightful wave that she felt herself floating on. It
was no less satisfying or diminished for her when it
was over...just different. And quite frankly, Chloe had
to admit, a vastly better sensation than what she
remembered from her youth with Harold. She
supposed it was just an indication of how much she
loved him now and how their relationship had
matured and grown over time. They lay together,
listening to the beating of each other's hearts against
the silence of the house, and Chloe never wanted it
to end.

However, it did, and without realizing it, they both
fell asleep soon after, reveling in the aftermath of their
emotions. The night was quiet and still, and within just
minutes after falling asleep, all that could be heard in
the room were their deep, steady exhalations.

* * *

HOWEVER, about an hour or so later, Chloe stirred as
she was awakened by an odd shuffling and bumping
around disturbance that seemed to be coming from the
ground level. She hesitated and listened again in case it
had just been some dream fragment that was still alive

in her brain. But as she cocked her head, there it was again.

"Harold!" she exclaimed in an urgent whisper. "Are you awake?"

"I am now. What's wrong?"

"I think I hear something or someone downstairs."

He leaned up on his elbows and listened, but all he heard was a light breeze squeezing around the stones of the mansion. "You sure? I don't hear anything."

"Wait…"

The sound started up again suddenly. It was muffled and softer now, eliminating the second floor as the source for sure.

"You hear it now?"

"Yeah. I do."

"Think we have an intruder?"

Harold shrugged as he tried to figure out a plan. He knew they were alone in the place since both Tony and Reggie had left for the night, and he could not imagine that either Adam or Katie would be up and about. Maybe a curious raccoon?

"I guess anything's possible, but more likely just Tony who forgot something and came back to get it."

"Well, Jonathan is in Boston for a few days, and that makes us responsible for the welfare of his family. You are probably right, but should we take a look just to make sure?"

"I suppose so. Get your robe and stay right behind me."

They tiptoed down the hallway and peeked in on Adam and Katie. They were both fast asleep, their prone forms illuminated by the nightlight between their beds. They were just as Chloe had left them when she had put them to bed.

"At least the kids are okay, and whatever it is didn't wake them," Chloe whispered as they silently closed the bedroom door and went back into the hall. "

Chloe did not voice what came to her next, but she could not help it after all the talk of the legend of William and Penelope Aberdeen.... *Has Penelope come for a visit?* On the other hand, Harold found his thoughts gravitating toward a more concrete and rational explanation of a burglar looking for a quick score in a house undergoing construction that might have some valuable items just lying around. He looked at her.

"Ghosts?" Chloe finally uttered.

18

MAY 2008

*H*arold did not laugh this off even though he was more skeptical about such possibilities than Chloe.

"I was thinking something a bit more serious."

Chloe blanched when he offered his explanation.

"Maybe we should just call the police?"

"We could, but by the time they get here, whoever it is may be long gone, and it's likely the sirens would scare them off anyway."

Harold tilted his head, indicating for her to follow him, as they moved as quietly as possible down the steps. He picked up an old piece of pipe left over from some of Tony's work and began to move down the corridor toward the noise which seemed to be coming and going now.

"Is this smart, Harold?"

He shrugged. "Probably not. Get ready to run and call for help if this goes south, okay?"

Chloe nodded and treaded just behind Harold as

they continued moving forward. The noise stopped suddenly. Just out of habit, Harold looked into each room they passed, but nothing seemed to be missing or even out of place.

"Think they heard us or maybe got what they wanted and left?"

"Beats me. Maybe we're getting all freaked over nothing and it's just some curious raccoon or something."

Chloe appreciated Harold trying to find the most innocuous or simple explanation just then, but in the back of her mind, she could not push away the images of what she had seen at her grandparent's farm in Luray, Virginia, when she had been just seven:

Chloe knew as well as anyone, even at her young age, that Luray was renowned for its vast system of underground caves and caverns, many of which had been commercialized for the public. But she and the kids she had made friends with over the years when she had visited knew of a secret and, as far as they knew, a yet-to-be-discovered cavern where they often went to explore and create games of their own. But on this one day, Chloe had not been able to round anyone up and headed off on her own with her grandfather's beloved basset hound, Rounder.

She went only with a flashlight and a light jacket to ward off the chill to the interior. At the time, her curiosity far outweighed any concerns of safety or danger, and she and Rounder found the entrance with no problem. She pushed aside the brush that she and her friends there had used to try to keep the opening as hidden as possible. They just saw it as their own private clubhouse and did not want any grown-

ups stumbling across it and sealing it off. Chloe clicked on the light and began the slow and careful descent into the cave with Rounder at her heels. They passed all the landmarks that Chloe knew well, and soon, the light from the opening was gone, and her only means of seeing anything was the flashlight.

Even now, she could not say what had possessed her to move farther inside—much farther than she had even ventured before—but it was like there was some unseen thing drawing her in. She finally got to the level part of the interior where she and her friends often set up to play and then walked on until she came to a spot where the path split into two directions. She shined the light to the right and saw that the tunnel was blocked from a collapse of the walls, just a few feet ahead. But the left option was not, and she moved inside it, panning her light all over the surfaces and along the floor so she did not trip on anything.

The tunnel proceeded for about another fifty yards or so until Chloe found herself in a large, almost perfectly circular room with a towering ceiling covered with thin, spindly stalactites. Water dripped from the sharp, pointed ends, and she slipped on her jacket to keep the water from chilling her too much. As well, the floor of the opening was spotted with the occasional stalagmite that she maneuvered her way around as she went across the space. Once she was about halfway across, she stopped and ran the light over everything around her.

The walls gleamed with water seeping from the rocks as well as being embedded with what looked to her like some blueish-white minerals that reflected her light back like small mirrors. It was the most incredible sight she had ever seen. But after a few moments, Chloe began to recall the collapsed tunnel she had gone by and thought it wise not to linger too much longer just in case the tunnel she had come down was just as unstable. Plus, she was by herself, and no one had any idea where she was. She called to Rounder, who had wandered over to sniff at a large pool of water that had formed in the back of the room.

The dog obediently came when he heard his name, but before they could take another step, Chloe froze in place as she was sure she heard the faint but unmistakable call of a voice. At first, she was sure it was just one of the neighborhood kids who had probably dropped by just as she had, but when she listened more closely, it was definitely not the voice of a child. Afraid that some adult had finally discovered their secret hideout, Chloe whispered to Rounder, and they took cover behind a large circular rock that had been smoothed to a glassy finish from years of water erosion.

Her heart pounded as she killed her light, and she and Rounder sat in the pitch dark to wait to see who would make an appearance. But as the seconds ticked by, no one seemed to be coming down the tunnel and headed their way. All she could hear as they hid was the beating of her own heart and Rounder's soft pants. Chloe relaxed and exhaled in relief, chiding herself for imagining things. She had been down here enough to know that the winds that made their way into the various passageways could play tricks on your ears. But as Chloe stood from her crouch and apologized to Rounder, playfully begging him not to tell anyone how childish she had been, a soft but growing light began to take shape between them and the way out.

Chloe kept the flashlight off as she stood and watched in

fascination and wonder as the orange-tinted light—more of a diffused mist of fog—began to take on an elongated shape until there, standing in front of her, was an older woman. Chloe was sure she was seeing things, but the longer she looked at the vision, the more she knew it had to be real. Though she had no explanation.

The light that was making up the woman's form dissolved away, and she began to wander the large room aimlessly as she called out in a desperate and anxious voice. Chloe shrank back, trying to conceal themselves again, and put a hand to Rounder's scruff as he began to whine and tremble. But the woman seemed so intent on her search that Chloe was sure she had no idea they were even there. From when she had been old enough to understand anything, Chloe had eavesdropped on the late-night conversations in her grandparents' home when the adults sat around and told each other tales of rural Virginia that had been passed down for ages.

One of those stories, she remembered just then, was about this woman whose children has mysteriously disappeared into a cave one day and were never found again. The woman had been overcome with grief and anguish at their disappearances and, according to the legend, had thrown herself off a cliff to her death. Chloe looked over again from her hiding spot and saw the look of utter devastation and defeat on the woman's face as she wailed and howled in pain before collapsing in a heap on the ground.

Chloe was unsure, but somehow, she just knew this was the spirit of that woman still looking for her long-lost children. Up to that point, Chloe had never thought ghosts were anything but fables and myths, but this experience was changing all that. There was no doubt in her mind now that ghosts were indeed real. Not knowing why, she moved from behind the rock with Rounder at her side, closer to the apparition, letting her glow illuminate her path. She felt no fear. Only sadness and empathy for the poor lost woman.

But just as she was trying to move so the woman could get a glimpse of her, the woman's form began to waver and flicker, like when their TV got lousy reception, and she just dissolved to nothing as if she had been nothing more than low-lying fog on a humid morning on the farm. Rounder went over and sniffed the spot where the woman had collapsed and looked back at Chloe with a plaintive whine as she flipped on the flashlight. The spot was indeed empty, but unless Chloe was making up something in her own mind just to rationalize what she thought she had seen, sure enough, there at Rounder's front paws was an indentation in the loose soil.

Chloe collected Rounder, and they made their way back out of the cavern without further incident. She went back to the farm but never said anything about what had happened for fear of being teased and made fun of by the adults.

So as they approached the kitchen, where a weak light was now bleeding into the dark hallway, both Harold and Chloe tensed as whatever was going on was about to unfold and make itself known. For Harold, he raised the pipe in a tight grip, anticipating the confrontation of an intruder or worse. But to Chloe, after recalling that day back in Virginia, she was firmly preparing herself for coming face to face with the ghost of Penelope Aberdeen.

19

MAY 2008

*H*arold took a deep breath, reached just inside the kitchen doorframe, and felt around until he found the wall switch and flicked on the overhead light. The glow they had seen, drawing them there, had begun to come closer. He raised the section of pipe in his hand over his head and gripped it tightly in preparation for having to defend himself and Chloe against some intruder. But as the light flashed on, Harold found himself face to face with a middle-aged man, his hair graying at the temples, his arm wrapped around a flimsy cardboard box that looked as if it might disintegrate at any moment.

The man's eyes went wide, looking as startled and surprised as Harold was sure he felt at that second. He dropped the box as he backed away, holding up his arms in a defensive position before falling to his rear. Harold stood over him and bellowed.

"Stay right where you are, pal! Chloe, call 9-1-1!"

The man was breathing hard as he scrambled away

a few steps, pushing with his feet and sliding on his rear, still not sure that Harold wouldn't maim him with the heavy length of lead in his hand.

"Wait, wait!" he exclaimed in a tone of genuine fear and panic, "I can explain...please!"

Harold took a beat and looked into his eyes. He did not know why, but something there made him feel the man deserved a chance to talk. If this were a hardened criminal intent on fleecing Jonathan Thompson of some valuable artifacts, then he certainly was not what Harold had envisioned when they had begun to make their way downstairs.

"Hold on a second, Chloe," Harold said finally, still holding the pipe in its ready position in case he had misread the man's eyes, and this was a trick of some sort. "You've got thirty seconds, pal; talk!"

"Okay...okay...my name is Thompson...Danny Thompson. Jonathan's my brother."

Harold could not have been more surprised just then if the man had sprouted a horn and suddenly become a unicorn. But he remained cautious and on the defensive regardless. Even if this were Jonathan's brother, that did not mean he was not here to rob him. Who would know better, he supposed, than a brother just what was lying around for the taking.

"Make a believer out of me," Harold replied.

"Okay...sure, sure...Jonathan and his wife Teresa moved here a number of years back from New York and bought this old mansion to renovate. Two kids, Adam and Katie. Teresa was murdered about three years ago, and the crime was never solved. That good enough?"

Harold relaxed and lowered his arm. Those were enough details to convince him that his guy was possibly Jonathan's brother, though there was still the outside possibility that anyone around might know those detail as well. However, the man certainly posed no threat to them, and Harold offered his hand to help him to his feet.

"Okay, Danny, was it? You may or may not be telling me the truth. I mean, everyone in Green Pond probably knows all of that. Tell me something that maybe only you might know about your brother that's not public knowledge."

"Mind if I sit? I'm still shaking."

Harold nodded, and Danny fell heavily into a chair at the kitchen table as Harold kept a close watch on him. He took a few deep breaths and then told Harold a much more detailed and involved account of the brothers Thompson than Harold had really been expecting. He was finally convinced and set the pipe aside as he and Chloe sat at the table with Danny. Harold quickly explained who he and Chloe were and why they were staying at the mansion.

"Okay, so you're Jonathan's brother," Harold said, "so why are you skulking around down here in the middle of the night?"

"Yeah. Sorry about that. I had no idea anyone was here. Typically both Tony and Reggie have gone for the day by this late hour, and I thought the place would be empty."

That further reinforced Danny's story with Harold, but it still did not rule him out as some thief, maybe knowing Jonathan was out of town.

"So…maybe you thought an empty house would be the perfect time to clean it out?" Harold asked, still not convinced of what was going on.

"No, no…nothing like that. Let me explain."

"Please do," Chloe replied, making her presence known in case the man had thought her irrelevant.

Over the next few minutes, Danny Thompson laid out a heartfelt justification for his presence. He explained that ever since Teresa had been killed, it had been impossible for Jonathan to deal with and let go of many of the things that had belonged to her for sentimental reasons but that really served no other purpose. In fact, all they were realistically doing were constantly reminding him of her.

"I saw how he was struggling and would never be able to fully clear out the reminders of Teresa that needed to be out of his sight. I stepped in and offered to do this for him to try to help with his still-lagging recovery over her death. That's why I was here tonight. I got into Green Pond later than I had planned, and I wanted to get this done before Tony and his guys were milling around in the morning."

Harold nodded.

"Call him if you like. He'll confirm it."

"That's okay, Danny. I'm sure you're telling us the truth. Sorry about all of this tonight. It's just that we thought someone had broken in and….well…sorry…."

"No problem. I get it. Just a bad set of circumstances all around. No harm, no foul."

"How about some coffee?" Chloe asked.

"Have anything stronger? I'm still a bit shaky over almost getting clonked on the head."

Harold apologized again before pulling out an old bottle of scotch that Reggie had left behind from his latest food run. He poured them all a small dram, and they sat and talked to try to clear the air between them completely.

"You and Jonathan are close then?" Chloe asked as she sipped the burning drink.

"When we were kids, we were inseparable. I guess we skipped that whole sibling rivalry thing you hear about. Jonathan was my best friend in the world."

"You said *was*?" Harold probed.

"I should qualify that…I'm sure that sounded like we might be at odds now. Back when we were kids, as I said, we rarely were seen apart. We liked the same things and spent a lot of time just roaming the fields and forests outside the family property."

"Up in Maryland?" Chloe asked.

Harold suppressed a grin, appreciative that she was still not totally convinced of Danny's story and was testing him based on a tidbit they had gleaned from Jonathan during their interview.

"Yeah…really tiny place called Grantville, where Maryland, West Virginia, and Pennsylvania come together. You probably never heard of it."

Chloe nodded when this matched up with what Jonathan had told them.

"Never been there, but I know of it," she replied, "I grew up in Virginia."

"Anyway," Danny continued, "time went on, and when it was time for the two of us to make decisions about what we would do with our lives, we kind of lost touch for a long time. It was nothing bad or done in anger, but just one of those things that happen with guys separated by distance. As a rule, I have found men not to be the best at keeping in touch in that circumstance."

Chloe smiled and looked at Harold. He got her drift and made a mental note to do better at that with some old friends who had moved away from Hampton but had been close to him when they had lived there.

"I did my best at the time, but my job eventually took me overseas, and it just got harder and harder. Maybe I should have made a greater effort, but I didn't, and that was that. We just kind of drifted apart until recently."

"Teresa's murder?" Harold asked.

20

MAY 2008

*D*anny looked up with a pain in his eyes and nodded. "Partly. I got transferred back to Savannah, oddly enough, and her murder occurred just before I returned. I was on my way home when this email—from out of the blue—arrived from Jonathan. It had been so long since I had heard from him that I knew it must be an emergency of some sort. And when I read it…well…."

Harold and Chloe nodded their understanding as Harold gave them each a second helping of scotch.

"As you might imagine, I found Jonathan a complete wreck when I got to Green Pond. I got my business partners to cover for me for a few weeks while I helped him through the investigation and the memorial service. And right now, I've stepped in to do what I can to try to help make this place—and please forgive my crude way of putting this—as "Teresa-free" as possible so he can function when he's home between trips."

They both sat quietly and just nodded. Chloe was

thoroughly impressed with the character and devotion of this man to his brother. It reminded her of just how much each of her siblings back in Virginia still meant to her. Harold was not the only one, she told herself, who had been lackadaisical in staying in touch with those close to him.

"So that's what's going on with me, guys," Danny said as he sat back and sighed with fatigue. "I never married or had kids, but I know how much Teresa meant to him. And those kids…who could not feel for what they have been put through? I have been a fairly absent uncle for a long time, but I want to change all that."

Harold smiled thinly as he was similarly impressed with Danny Thompson. He had never had the bond of a brother, but he would like to think that if he had, he would have been one like Danny Thompson appeared to be for Jonathan.

"It's wonderful that you can step up to try to help Jonathan get back on his feet, Danny," Chloe replied. "And I'm sure your presence with Adam and Katie will help as well."

"I hope so, too. They really took another blow when that pathetic excuse of a nanny Jonathan hired just up and split without so much as a word to anyone. For Jonathan, it was bad enough, but those kids are still pretty fragile following their mother's death. It was like they were being abandoned all over again."

"You heard the reason she took off?" Harold asked.

Danny nodded. "Bunch of crap, in my opinion," he replied.

"You not familiar with the legend of the Aberdeens?" Chloe asked.

"Oh…it's hard to be in Green Pond for any length of time and not know about that myth. Let's just say I have never experienced anything that would make me believe that such things like that happened here…or anywhere else for that matter."

Chloe nodded and said nothing, keeping her own beliefs to herself, knowing they would only cause friction. Right now, it seemed as if Danny Thompson were a gift to his brother and the circumstances, and she did not want to do anything to cut that off.

"I'm sorry, but to do that to children—any children—is inexcusable," Danny added as he took a drink.

"Was she the only help he had with the kids since Teresa's death?" Chloe asked, trying to cool his conversational tone.

"No, there were others. Though my brother and I grew up close and tight, he's nothing like me personality-wise. You might have noticed that Jonathan is not exactly what you would call warm and fuzzy." He laughed quietly as he said that, and Harold and Chloe smiled.

"It's okay to agree. Jonathan has always been like that, even before losing Teresa. I was the gregarious and outgoing one which led me to what I do for a living. But Jonathan was…well…I guess more serious and introspective is the best way to describe him. He was never rude or mean, but just was more of a 'let's get to the point' kind of guy."

"That was my impression," Harold said.

"He tried several nannies following Teresa's death, but his personality can be quite off-putting to some, and I think it made a few of them uncomfortable. I got the feeling that they thought they were not doing the job he really wanted done or that he did not like them for some reason. It was really hard for Jonathan to be sociable and chatty in the aftermath. Put that on top of his true personality, and well...you get the idea."

"How about the most recent one?" Chloe asked. "Did you get the feeling she felt like that about him as well?"

"She was here so briefly that it's hard to say. Seemed like she had no business taking the job in the first place...like she just needed a gig and it didn't matter what it was."

"Tony mentioned that she seemed a bit fragile and shaky from day one," Harold replied.

"Yeah, I'd say that's pretty accurate. The Aberdeen legend was just the excuse she was looking for to run away, I think."

"That's what Tony said," Chloe added.

"I always wondered if she was running from something else when she arrived here. It was just a feeling I got. Anyway, it was no excuse for what she did to Adam and Katie."

"Have you been able to get back to your own life after stepping in to support Jonathan and the kids?" Harold asked.

"Actually, I have. My partners were really understanding and sympathetic, and we have worked out an arrangement that will allow me to get up here to Green Pond a day or two each week just to keep an eye out."

"Your brother is still reeling, even after three years?" Chloe asked.

Danny shrugged and looked her in the eye. "Everyone heals in their own way and in their own time."

"I'm sorry. I didn't mean anything by that. It's just that it's admirable that you have dropped your own life to do this is all."

"It's okay. I think, for the most part, Jonathan is getting better each day, but every once in a while, I see signs that he's slipping backward. I'm worried about him having some major relapse and want to do all I can to keep that from happening."

"Hence your trip here tonight?" Harold interjected.

"Exactly. The sooner I get some of these more sensitive items out of this space, the better. You know the old saying, 'out of sight out of mind?'"

They nodded.

"He was really in bad shape when you got back?" Chloe asked with a deep tone of concern.

"You have no idea," Danny replied. "For a while there, I wasn't sure he was going to make it."

They both had no idea exactly what Danny meant by that last comment, but it was really none of their business. The man was an altruistic knight, and they felt as if they pulled more than was necessary out of him, making him go back through the nightmare he had walked into.

"Even now, when he is much better, he's become a

virtual recluse here. Jonathan doesn't seem to ever go out unless he's traveling for business. And that, on top of his innate personality, he just doesn't have the skills necessary to nurture and care for the kids like Teresa did. Plus, I think to some degree, it still pains him to just be here in the place where Teresa died. He still blames himself for being away when it happened."

"Well, that's where we come in, I guess," Harold replied.

"I sure hope so, guys," Danny said as he finished off his drink and put the glass on the table, "I sure hope so."

21

MAY 2008

K nowing they had kept Danny long enough and that they needed to get some sleep as their first day on the job needed to set a good impression, Harold and Chloe bid Danny goodnight.

"Again, guys, so sorry for freaking you out and scaring the pants off you."

"No problem, Danny," Harold replied as he shook his hand warmly. "It's on us as well."

"Tell you what," Danny went on, "I'll be around a bit here even with you guys on board now, and please feel free to contact me anytime if you have questions or concerns that Tony might not have a handle on. I'd be happy to drop by or talk to you, especially when you're just getting settled in and oriented to the place and your new jobs, okay?"

"That's great, Danny," Chloe said, "and very kind."

Danny pulled out his wallet and handed Harold a business card. "You can call my office or my cell anytime. Thanks again for showing up just when we needed someone. I'm sure things will begin to take a big swing upward for Jonathan now. I can sense you're the perfect people for him."

They walked him out and watched him drive away.

"Well, after a brief fright, that was an extraordinary experience," Harold said as he put his arm around Chloe's waist.

"I'll say. You don't come along people as devoted and dedicated to their families as that every day."

* * *

HAROLD AND CHLOE rose with an odd combination of fuzzy fatigue and excitement as the sun slanted across the bed the next morning. They both knew they would likely pay the price for staying up so late and chatting up Danny Thompson as the day wore on, but right now, the feeling of the unknown and the challenge of this new adventure overrode all of that. Plus, it was hard to ignore the enticing aroma of coffee and frying bacon that made its way up the staircase and into their bedroom. Not wanting to have anyone think them unable to answer the bell to service, they both got up as if on autopilot and prepared for the day as quickly as possible.

The smells coming from Reggie's breakfast were just as alluring the closer they got to the kitchen, and he had plates waiting for them as they sat. It was like the man had some sort of X-ray vision, Harold thought, knowing just when to serve food up without having it sit around and get cold. After eating a filling breakfast of the most delectable and fluffy pancakes with crisp, succulent bacon on the side, Harold had him pour off a new serving of the rich coffee that had come along with the breakfast as he stood to go find Tony.

"You really ready for this, Chloe?"

"Absolutely. See you at dinner, I'm guessing?"

Harold nodded and kissed her goodbye before giving Reggie a serious high-five and savoring the aroma of the to-go coffee he knew would be needed to keep his engine running just then.

"The kids already eat, Reggie?" Chloe asked as she got a refill on her coffee as well.

"They did. Despite it all, they're early risers and are likely back up in their room, entertaining themselves. They have kind of been left to their own devices since the last nanny took off."

"Well, I guess it's time to try to set up some sort of routine for them to get them back on track, huh?"

Reggie just smiled as he collected the dirty dishes and went to the sink to begin the clean-up.

"Wonderful breakfast, Reggie. You know, if I were in the market for a wife, I would be sorely tempted about you with meals like you have been preparing for us."

Reggie howled with laughter. "Thanks, Chloe, that's a very intriguing offer. Have a great day!"

* * *

As Chloe headed back to the staircase to check on Adam and Katie, Harold found Tony out back, sitting at a table with the two workers who had not cut and run on him when the tales of Penelope Aberdeen's ghost had spread. Harold joined them, and Tony introduced everyone.

"Okay, guys," Tony said to the men, "you need anything more, come find me, but for now, just focus on those loose roof tiles that got peeled away during that last storm."

They nodded and headed off.

"Okay, boss, what's on tap for us today?"

Tony looked at him slyly. "Boss?"

"Aw, I'm just kidding, but you're calling the shots, just to be clear."

"Good enough, funny man. Okay, for the next couple of days, I want to get as much of the remaining exterior work done as we can. The forecast is good for the time being, but summers here can bring unexpected storms with little warning."

"Just like Hampton," Harold replied.

"I made up a rudimentary list of stuff I think we'll need for the projects on tap. From our discussions, I'm sure you know what will be needed as well. Look it over, and if you can think of anything I omitted, just add it on. Then head on into town and find Charley Needles at Green Pond Hardware. He knows you're coming and has already started getting stuff together for us."

"That small place in town? They going to have all these items?"

"Don't let the size of Charley's place fool you. I thought the same thing when I first began to work with him as well. I have no idea how he does it, but I have never gone there when he has not somehow filled all my needs with no excuses."

"Will do. See you as soon as I get back."

* * *

As Harold drove down the gravel drive and toward town, Chloe moved down the hallway and found Adam and Katie in the middle of the floor, completely absorbed in a game of some sort that seemed to be of their own invention. Chloe knew she would have to handle this situation with kid gloves to make any real progress with them. Diving in immediately and trying to begin lessons would be a waste of everyone's time and likely counterproductive in getting them to trust and feel comfortable around her. After all, at this point, they still did not even really know her. She just waved warmly when they looked up upon her arrival, and she sat off to the side and just watched them play.

They seemed unaffected by her presence and picked up right where they had left off. Chloe just sat and observed, and after a few minutes, she began to get the gist of this game, though the rules and regulations seemed to be very freeform and often modified as the game progressed. Sensing them getting more used to her being there, Chloe decided it was time to begin.

"Got room for another player?" she asked.

Katie smiled at her and scooted over so Chloe could

sit between them. For her first few "moves" in the game, Chloe just followed suit as best she could, and soon it was like she was just another one of them. She felt some of the wall that she had sensed initially between herself and them begin to lift. As the game progressed, Chloe slowly and surreptitiously began to try to chat them up a bit to get a better sense of just how much work might be facing her in breaking through completely. The kids did interact with her, but their answers still tended to be short and clipped. Their initial shyness and introverted behavior were definitely going to be her first challenges.

Otherwise, though, Adam and Katie appeared to be just normal kids that age, often laughing and shouting in glee when a successful outcome in the game came their way. With their focus on the game and having let her into their secluded world, Chloe began to ask questions to see if they might open up more to her about what had happened and how they felt about it. Using her training from college as well as some things she had learned from Dr. Abrams, Chloe floated inquiries here and there without making it sound like she was interrogating them or trying to make them feel on the spot with this new stranger who had landed in their lives.

22

MAY 2008

*C*hloe held her breath as she began, hoping she was not moving too quickly with them. She knew she was facing several hurdles here: being a stranger to them, dealing with kids who had been through horrific trauma, and then abandoned by one nanny after another. But as she pitched a question or two, her technique of making it seem like they were just chatting as friends seemed to be working. The kids never ignored her questions, but more times than not, they skirted around her inquiries, not directly addressing anything they might have seen or heard on that awful night. For Chloe, she was not at all surprised at that development. A brief talk with Cynthia Abrams had prepared her for this, with her therapist warning her that people coming through a really severe trauma often did any manner of things not to face up to the event itself...at least until they were ready.

When she saw that was getting her nowhere, she just pivoted a bit to get a sense of how they felt living in the mansion and what their lives were like on a daily basis. Initially, that tactic was met with the same resistance, but then in an unexpected turn of events, Katie began to open up more. But what she had to say caught Chloe off-guard and made her wonder if she was really prepared to help these kids recover. She sat silent and curious as Katie began to describe in some detail the "friends" who would come by the mansion from time to time to visit and play with her and Adam. Chloe knew from everyone at Aberdeen Estates that the kids had little, if any, contact with children from the town, so that revelation was confusing.

"You mean kids from town come out here to play?" Chloe asked as she took her move in the game.

"No," Katie replied happily, "these are special friends just for us."

That was when it dawned on Chloe that Katie was referring to a phase she herself had gone through when she had been about Katie's age. Despite her large family, Chloe had sometimes referred to her imaginary friends when no one was around. She was sure that was what Katie meant.

"Do you see them, too, Adam?" she asked.

"Yeah, sure. Sometimes," he replied as he took one of Katie's pieces in a surprise capture.

"No fair!" his sister protested vehemently.

"You forgot to ring the pincher!" Adam retorted back.

Chloe had no idea what ringing the pincher was— maybe a new rule had just been instituted—in any case, the dispute was dropped, and it seemed to have no impact on them talking about these imaginary friends. Chloe knew that creating imaginary friends was no big deal for kids, having been through a trauma or not, but in this case, she decided asking a bit more might be a good idea.

"What do they look like, Katie…these friends of yours?"

Katie took her next turn as she described in detail what their visitors looked like, including their clothes, etc. To Chloe, it all sounded a bit off unless their imaginations were so finely honed that they had created a vast array far beyond anything Chloe had ever dreamt up as a child.

"These the kids you saw, Adam?" Chloe asked, wondering if they each had their own separate friends.

"Some, but Katie has more than me…bunch of girlie stuff I don't like sometimes."

Chloe almost laughed but held it in, not wanting to make them think she was laughing at them. The game went on for a few more minutes with no more elaboration on this revelation as Chloe wrote it off as just a coping mechanism for them. But just seconds later, she felt a shiver run up her spine when Adam spoke up, shocking Chloe to her core.

"You gonna tell her about seeing Momma?" Adam asked without looking away from the game.

Katie shrugged. "Sure, I guess…sometimes Momma comes to see us as well."

Chloe did not know what to say. After a beat, she plowed ahead, just to make sure she had not misunderstood them. "Are you guys telling me your mother comes to your room to visit?" Chloe asked, trying to sound as if this was no big deal.

"Not a lot, but sometimes," Katie replied. "Maybe three or four times a year, right, Adam?"

"Something like that."

"Does she ever talk to you or touch you?" Chloe asked, dreading the answer.

"No, she just kind of sits there and looks over at us."

"Like she's checking to make sure you're okay?" Chloe asked.

"I guess," Adam replied. "That's it! I just bagged your biscuit! Game over!"

Chloe was startled until she realized he was referring to the game again.

"Let's go again!" Katie exclaimed.

Chloe looked at her watch and saw it was just after noon. "How about we take a break, guys. I'm pretty sure Reggie has your lunch ready. Maybe pick it up again after we eat?"

They both nodded and put away all the miscellaneous pieces that had been assembled for the game and stored them in a small cardboard box that went into the toy chest before running off to the kitchen. Chloe sat in place, wondering what in the hell was going on here.

While the kids rested, Chloe wandered down to the solarium and pondered all the events of her first morning with Adam and Katie. On the plus side, she seemed to have broken through at least the outer layer of the proactive bubble they had erected around themselves against the outside world. *But on the other side of the coin, what exactly is going on with what they claim to be seeing? Is this just some highly creative imagination at work that a lot of kids use, or is there something more at play?* If it had not been for her experience with the paranormal as a young girl and then the Aberdeen ghost story on top of that, Chloe might have believed the former. But the fact that Adam seemed to be seeing at least some of the same "friends" as Katie seemed to rule that out. And the big clincher of seeing their mother...if that were real and not just a child missing a mother and creating her out of thin air to cope, then the mansion had some real issues.

If Penelope Aberdeen really is still roaming the halls of Aberdeen Estates, then has Teresa Thompson joined the fray? Does she feel compelled to keep an eye on her kids from the other side? Or is she letting her belief in such things make her want ghosts to be here when they really are not?

23

MAY 2008

*M*eanwhile, down in Green Pond, Harold made the rounds to collect everything on the list Tony had come up with for their workweek. Just as he had predicted, Charley Needles had been able to fill the list save a few random items that he had prearranged for Harold to grab elsewhere in town. All he had to do was make a couple more stops and he would be done. At the hardware store and during his other errands, Harold began to bump into and meet a few more people from Green Pond. Initially, they were all friendly and welcoming; some even joked that they could not imagine why anyone would leave the "big city" of Hampton to come to Green Pond. Harold laughed along with them, but the air suddenly went colder when he went on to explain that he and his wife were working at the Aberdeen Estates to help with the renovation and take care of Jonathan's kids while he traveled.

"So you don't know about what went on out there, buddy?" one man finally asked.

"If you mean Teresa Thompson's murder, yeah…we know all about that."

"I'm not so sure you do, my friend."

"Oh?" Harold asked.

"The police, they never found the killer, but everyone here in Green Pond knows what happened."

"Really? Did you tell the police?"

"Well, I can't actually prove it, you see, but we know all the same."

"Mind if I ask what *did* happen, seeing as how I'm working out there?"

He shrugged. "Sure…old Jonathan says he was out of town on business when his wife got murdered, but lots of us here are not so sure. It's a well-known fact that Jonathan and Teresa Thompson did not get on all that well, despite how they appeared in town. There was supposedly this big blow-up right before her murder when he was allegedly away. We reckon he pretended to go away and then snuck back later to do the deed himself or just hired someone to do it for him. Man's got more money than God anyway."

"But no one ran this idea by the detectives during the investigation?"

"No idea. Thompson likely paid them off, in my opinion."

Harold walked off after hearing that wild conspiracy theory, but before he got out of Green Pond, he found out that belief was not just one held by a few. More than a handful of residents expressed a similar view to the man who had told him the story, making Harold begin to wonder if maybe there might be some validity to it after all. *Jonathan is still seemingly distraught and disturbed over Teresa's death, but what do they really know about the man?* He showed no real emotion or reaction to her death other than a cold and gruff demeanor when the topic came up. But then again, Danny had said that was just how his brother was. Harold was not normally open to conspiracies as a rule, but if their relationship were, in fact, troubled, then Jonathan Thompson certainly had the means and motive to end her life.

Could the story of how he is still grieving be just a façade? Was Thompson, despite his no-nonsense exterior, a capable enough actor to pull this off? Maybe the locals are onto something that is just lacking physical evidence. Or has there been evidence and it has been bribed away? It was all making Harold's head spin. He picked up the last item on Tony's list and headed back to the mansion with more questions than answers. All of a sudden, despite his assurances to Chloe, Harold had some serious anxiety over this decision regarding their safety. *And the biggest one of all is that he might have unwittingly walked them into something way more lethal in their rush to remove themselves from their own trauma.*

HAROLD RETURNED to the mansion and pulled the truck around back where he met Tony and his guys to begin unloading the materials he had picked up in town.

"Any trouble getting everything?" Tony asked as Harold closed his door and move to the bed to help unpack.

"Nope. Just like you said, Charley had it all under control."

They worked a bit longer when Tony pulled Harold aside out of the earshot of his workers.

"You okay, Harold?"

"Sure, why?"

"Looks like you've got something on your mind, is all."

Harold hesitated before saying anything about what he had learned from some of the locals in town but then decided it would not hurt just to get it off his chest. "Well, I ran into a few locals while I was picking stuff up, and several of them had an interesting theory on Teresa Thompson's murder."

"Let me guess, you ran into Ralph Yardley?"

"Yeah. You know about him and what he thinks happened out here with Teresa?"

"Oh, old Ralph will peddle that story to anyone kind enough to patronize him. I wouldn't give it too much weight. Kind of like the old Aberdeen legend, it's just another myth that has made its way around Green Pond. Our residency is aging here, and sometimes people just have too much time on their hands, you know?"

Harold nodded but did not offer up that Ralph Yardley was not the only one he had heard the same story from. "Okay. It just kind of caught me by surprise and felt really odd based on my impressions of Jonathan so far, is all."

"I would agree. I have been working pretty close here with him for a long time, Harold, and trust me, that conspiracy theory is complete bullshit. Don't lose any sleep over it, okay?"

Harold nodded but could not let go of it completely. From personal experience, he knew people often were very adept at showing a public mask while hiding who they really were. Maybe once he got to know Jonathan better and got a better sense of the mansion's big picture, he would agree with Tony. But for now, he was not so sure. He and Tony went over the priority schedule again, and Harold prepared for a full afternoon of work after grabbing a quick sandwich that Reggie had left for him in the kitchen.

MEANWHILE, Chloe sat quietly, eating her own lunch with Adam and Katie in the kitchen as she mulled over the various revelations that had come her way that morning. The imaginary friends issue was easy to accept, as she had done that when young. But telling her that they had actually seen a vision of Teresa was not so easy to shrug off. If it had been just one or the other, Chloe might have seen it as just a coping mechanism for an emotionally damaged child. But both Adam and Katie said they had seen her. Though Chloe's knowledge of such psychological phenomena was very limited, that seemed as if it might have another explanation altogether.

And she certainly was aware that her sensitivity to some paranormal event was coloring her perceptions, so she tried to keep that in mind as well. Maybe, she told herself, she could run the situation by Cynthia the next time they had their regularly scheduled phone session to get her take on it. She would be better trained in what else it might mean. But for now, she decided to just cope with this new information as best she could and not let it affect the great initial progress she felt she had made with both kids. None of it seemed to be of concern to either Adam and Katie, as Chloe watched them laugh and joke with each other as well as with her as they ate. It was a bright spot for Chloe in her interactions with them and one that she had not expected to see so soon. Adam and Katie were beginning to show glimpses and hints of being on their way back.

24

MAY 2008

*A*s a break for them all, Chloe decided maybe the kids would enjoy an afternoon hike in the woods bordering the property. They had been cooped up all day so far, and she figured some time out in nature might be another step in the right direction for strengthening a bond between herself and them. Certainly, the kids could use some exercise, and for herself, Chloe was hoping some fresh air and movement would get her mind off apparitions, ghosts, and the old legend of Aberdeen Estates that had raised her anxiety level since taking the job. Both Adam and Katie seemed thrilled to get out, and they even told her of a nice loop trail they knew of that went into the woods and circled around a small lake nearby.

Chloe threw some bottles of water as well as light jackets for all three of them into a small daypack she had brought from home, and they set off, the sun warm on their shoulders. The kids set a brisk pace, and Chloe found herself having to hustle to keep up. Long gone, she thought as she smiled to herself, were the days when she had this level of energy. After a few minutes, they passed into the cover of the thick trees, and the sun only filtered through here and there where the heavy leaves allowed.

Chloe had them stop every so often and quizzed them on the scant knowledge of plants and small insects she recalled from her few science classes in college they came upon so as to ease into some education as well. Fortunately, most of what they saw were well-known species, and it was only once or twice that Chloe had to admit she did not know what they were looking at. Amazingly to her, both kids knew quite a bit and even identified some things Chloe had no idea of. Everyone had been right. Deep down, these were bright and outgoing children. After a quick water break, they came upon the lake that Adam and Katie had told her about, and they found a wide, flat rock at the water's edge to sit on and rest.

It was an unremarkable pond, Chloe thought, but pretty and alluring in its own right. The kids squealed with delight when a frog would suddenly leap from a hiding spot into the water, or a lurking fish would rise to the surface to snag a bug or two. It was relaxing and just the break Chloe had been shooting for when she had suggested the outing. But her mind was still abuzz with everything from the morning, and she was finding it hard to truly enjoy the afternoon as much as the kids seemed to be. Her muscles appreciated the exercise, but her mind was just refusing to come along for the ride.

The only way she knew to try to make sense of all

of it was to run it by Harold once their day was over. He might have some insight on it all, not having been in the room with the kids when all was revealed. Plus, she knew, though he was not a hardcore skeptic on the subject, he was way more objective in his view of the paranormal and might be able to make her see that she was just putting too much emphasis on a supernatural explanation. As the sun began to head down to the tree line and a light breeze picked up to create a small ripple across the lake, Chloe collected the kids, and they headed back home.

DINNER FROM REGGIE was another hit with all, and by the time Chloe and Harold pushed away from their plates, she had no idea how she was ever going to be able to go back to doing her own cooking again once they went home to Hampton. Even the kids seemed to devour it all, reinforcing Reggie's earlier note that they were not picky eaters. That was a new one for Chloe with kids of this age, herself included, as she recalled.

"Where did you learn to cook like this, Reggie?" Harold asked as he offered to help him collect the dishes and take them to the kitchen sink.

"Sit tight, Harold. I got this."

"Just force of habit, I guess."

Chloe hit him playfully in the arm as they all laughed.

"To answer your question, I guess it began with my mom down in Baton Rouge."

"So that's where that accent is from!" Chloe exclaimed

"That it is...anyway, I just kind of hung around in my mom's kitchen. She ran a small café in town, and when they saw I had a real talent for it, I went away to culinary school."

"Lucky for us," Harold said with a grin. "How did you end up in Green Pond?"

"Oh, one thing led to another, and then I met Mr. Thompson. It's been a great relationship ever since, and I guess Green Pond is really my home now."

Harold could see something in his eyes that made him know there was way more to this story than Reggie was willing to divulge. But he also knew when to stop pushing with someone who obviously did not want to elaborate on something or was uncomfortable talking about it, and he just nodded.

"Thanks again, Reggie," Chloe interjected when the lag in conversation began to get odd.

"My pleasure, Chloe."

As Reggie bustled around the table, Chloe gathered Adam and Katie and headed upstairs to get them set for bed.

"Want to talk about your day when you are done, Chloe?" Harold asked.

"That would be great! Meet you on the back patio in...say twenty minutes?"

"Perfect."

Chloe herded a much more upbeat version of the kids, wondering how Harold knew she needed to talk. She did not think she had been sending out any signals in that regard, but then again, ever since she had met Harold, he had always seemed to know. She found Harold on the patio with a bottle of wine and two glasses as a slim sliver of moon hung over the back-yard. She sat and exhaled in relief that the day was finally over. He poured them both a glass, and they clinked glasses before sipping.

"How did you know I needed to talk about the day?"

Harold grinned. "I suppose I could claim some newfound clairvoyance or the sudden development of ESP, but it's none of that."

"So...."

"First of all, I can't imagine that your first day in this new role is not worth hearing about. But mostly, those kids are not the same closed-off, shy creatures they were just twenty-four hours ago. There has to be a story behind that!"

Chloe laughed and shook her head, amazed at how perceptive Harold continued to be with her. He sat back as she launched into all that had happened with her and the kids that day. She began with how surpris-ingly easy it had been to get them to accept her when she just inserted herself in their game as if she was a friend and not some new rule-enforcer. But she watched with entertainment and amusement as he absorbed her recounting of the kids' imaginary friends as well as the occasional visit from Teresa Thompson. She left nothing out, including her own take on it. She knew that while Harold did not view paranormal events as pure fantasy, as Jonathan and his brother did, he had an analytically skeptical view of them.

"Am I way off base here? Making too much out of some children's imaginations?" she asked when she was done.

Harold paused and sipped at his wine as he chose his response. "Interesting day, Chloe," he replied with a furrowed brow.

"Yeah, but what do you think?"

"Well, you know my stand on this stuff, right? I'm still on the fence with it all, but this sighting of Teresa —from both of them, not just Adam or Katie alone— makes me wonder if my belief system is due for a tweaking. The imaginary friend thing I can write off as a child's normal development, but the dead mother… not so much."

"So you think Teresa Thompson could actually be in residence here for some reason?"

"Funny you should ask that. When I tell you the bomb that got dropped on me in town today, I think you may get an answer."

25

MAY 2008

$\mathcal{C}$hloe sat slack jawed as Harold filled her in on what old Ralph Yardley had told him regarding what he believed to be the truth surrounding the murder of Teresa Thompson.

"So he thinks this was all some elaborate scheme by Jonathan to rid himself of a wife he might have been having a troubled relationship with and then got the police to cover it all up for him?" she replied in a hushed voice so they would not be overheard.

"In a nutshell, that seems to be the consensus opinion."

"Consensus? You mean…"

"Yep…Ralph was not the only one I heard this from…or at least a similar version of anyway."

"But what is the motive? I mean, Jonathan is the one with the money. Unless there was some affair going on or something."

"True. Money and sex are the normal motivators in such things, at least from thriller novels I read. But who knows what was really going on with them behind closed doors? I mean, what do we *really* know about Jonathan anyway?"

"He sure seemed broken up over her death, though, and Danny indicated it nearly destroyed him."

Harold nodded. "From my perspective, Jonathan Thompson doesn't appear to be acting, but again, who knows? He might be so good at this that he has even pulled the wool over his brother's eyes."

Chloe sat back and took a sip before looking long and hard at Harold. "You thinking we might have stepped into a hornet's nest here?"

"The thought did occur to me."

"Yikes."

Harold nodded as they both went silent and just sipped as the moon rose higher and the stars overhead began to multiply dramatically. Nothing more was discussed between them that evening regarding what they had shared with one another. However, their former mood of excitement and eagerness to get their own lives back on track had suddenly been tempered and overshadowed and tainted with a feeling of concern, anxiety, and regret. The warm and pleasant evening abruptly felt too close and heavy all around them. It was like this invisible dome had been placed over the mansion and was closing in on them. There was little they could think of to stop it, short of just packing up and running away as well.

* * *

HAROLD AND CHLOE retired as soon as they had polished off the bottle of wine. It had been a long day for both of them—in more ways than one—but after Chloe lay down, she just could not find the sleep she knew she desperately needed after having a short night on Sunday. In any other circumstances, she might have blamed the excess of wine for her restlessness. It was common with her and why she did not drink all that much these days, but her current situation was far from normal. Every time she closed her eyes, all she could see were alternating images of the apparition of Teresa Thompson floating through the hallways of the mansion with the hideous experience she had been through back in Hampton.

It had been a long time since she had been plagued with issues from losing the baby—in fact, since she had been seeing Dr. Abrams regularly, that part of her trauma had just faded away. But now they were back. The few moments when she was able to drop off to sleep, a series of images came flying at her faster than she could count regarding her lost child. Some were replays of what had actually happened, including the horror of reliving those dreadful hours in the ER, while others were things that had never happened at all. The latter were exaggerations and creations—from her subconscious, she guessed—that made her bolt upright in tears.

The interplay between the two nightmares was curious, and Chloe tried to understand if it were, in fact, that the revelation of Teresa appearing in the mansion to Adam and Katie that had somehow caused her old trauma dreams to return. The images that came to her were so real it was not until she was fully awake and able to catch her breath that she could discern her dreams from her waking reality next to Harold. The one plus was that in all her thrashing about and tossing and turning, she had somehow not managed to wake him, though she had no idea how he had slept through it all. She tried one more time, but found herself too hot, then too cold, the just too anxious and antsy to calm her mind enough to just relax.

Afraid by that point to even close her eyes again for fear of having the whole cycle recur, Chloe got up and walked the empty halls and rooms of the upper floor of the mansion, trying to make sense of it all. It was only when she had reached the staircase a second time and was about to descend that what Harold had told her from Ralph Yardley began to sink in and form a clearer bigger picture of the situation. From reading, she had learned that spirits often felt compelled to remain in the place where they had a violent end to their physical lives or were taken before their natural timeline came to an end. In this case, that seemed to explain the appearance of Teresa Thompson—if she had, in fact, been real—perfectly.

Everyone had made it clear that little in the world meant more to Teresa than Adam and Katie, and they had been ripped from her by her premature death. Why this had happened was still all theory and speculation, as there was still no hard physical evidence anywhere to point to her killer. But regardless of the who and the why, Chloe now firmly believed that

Teresa was still there out of love and concern for the kids. *But now, if the story Harold came back to the mansion with is true, then is Teresa perhaps looking for help identifying and bringing her killer to justice?* Chloe knew this was her creative and imaginative mind at play, but she could not help wondering all the same.

And Harold did have a point. They knew very little about Jonathan Thompson. They just knew him based on a very brief interview and what they had gotten from those who knew him better. Everyone had reiterated how much he loved the kids, but when she thought back, no one had said much about how he really felt about Teresa. The only comment they had to go on was that there had been some friction between them from time to time and reports of a bigger blow-up just before she was killed. *But did that really mean anything significant? I mean, what marriage does not have spats and squabbles from time to time?* Even she and Harold, as solid a relationship as she felt they had, had certainly been marked with an argument or two. *Would that make someone from the outside who heard them argue think it serious enough to think Harold might go crazy and kill her?*

Chloe shook her head, knowing she was letting her thoughts run wild on way too little corroborated information—small-town gossip was hardly adequate. *So, where does that leave her?* She did not know. When she had gotten up to try to calm her racing mind, all she had done was make it worse. The walking and guessing and trying to formulate a real assessment of who had murdered Teresa Thompson, and more importantly, why, was just creating more questions. The big sticking point in her craw, though, was that from what she *did* know, it made no sense for Jonathan to have been the killer unless there was some sort of sexual dalliance involved that no one but Teresa and Jonathan and the third member of some love triangle might be aware of.

She realized that finding that out might never be revealed, especially if an affair were being conducted during Jonathan's so-called business trips. There had been this guy Harold had done work for early in his career who had done just that. He traveled extensively, and then one day, by sheer chance and through the magic of electronic communication, his wife had found out he had been having long-term, intimate relationships with different women in every city he was traveling to. He did not seem the type to Chloe—certainly, his brusk demeanor was a key to argue against that— but then again, she supposed anyone was capable if tempted enough and was not especially happy at home.

As that notion came to her, Chloe found herself wandering the lower corridor and decided enough was enough. She was letting her thoughts run wild when what she needed was sleep. Maybe some warm milk or just a simple glass of water would do the trick. But as she cleared her thoughts and moved forward, she slowed, hearing a muted voice coming from one of the side rooms in the hall. She knew the voice but just could not place it. *Who is that? And more importantly, why are they up in the middle of the night, carrying on some seemingly secretive conversation?*

26

MAY 2008

*E*ven with all that had transpired in the last day or so, Chloe could not help quell her curiosity as to why someone would be on the phone in the middle of the night, obviously trying to keep whatever it was they were talking about to themselves. Not only was it an odd hour to be doing that, but the voice seemed to be purposefully hushed as if the conversation needed to be private. She crept along, inch by inch, as she concentrated harder on identifying the voice that sounded so familiar yet just out of the grasp of her memory.

Reggie was ruled out right away due to his accent, but then again, he had left hours ago, and even considering him was ludicrous. Another possibility, of course, was Tony, but the timbre and cadence were completely different from Tony's way of talking...and besides, *why in the hell would Tony come back to the mansion to make a call when he has his own house just a half of a mile or so yards away?* That left only Danny and Jonathan...but she recalled that Danny had had this subtle but hard-to-miss lisp when he pronounced diphthongs. The man talking had a clear and concise speech delivery. In her fatigued mind and the slight pall of fear hanging over her from her eavesdropping, Chloe suddenly knew it *had* to be Jonathan.

She chastised herself for not recognizing his voice earlier, but he had not been on her initial list of possibilities because Jonathan was out of town…. *Isn't he?* She stopped briefly and thought back. *That's right.* Jonathan had made a big deal of letting Tony know he was on his way to Boston and to make sure she and Harold got paid if he got held up. *So…why is Jonathan in his study on the phone?* Chloe furrowed her brow, trying to make sense of this, but then again, maybe she had just misunderstood and he had not left town yet. However, since she and Harold had talked, her suspicion and uncertainty surrounding Jonathan were in the front of her brain now, and that overrode the possibility that she had misunderstood…*no!* He was definitely leaving from that last meeting with everyone.

With that realization firmly in place, Chloe's insatiable curiosity took over, and she moved closer to the office door that was just slightly ajar to see if she could pick up any tidbits that might clarify who the real Jonathan Thompson was…assuming he was maybe not the person Danny and Tony thought he was…that maybe the group of locals who thought he had been responsible for Teresa's death were on to something after all. His voice was definitely low and guarded, and though she could only hear his side of the conversation, his normally cool and reserved personality seemed a bit heated and urgent as he talked.

Chloe crept as close to the opening as she dared and then did her best to keep her breathing quiet so she would not be detected. She leaned in and heard what sure sounded like a very pointed and pressing situation. It was hard to say exactly all of what was being discussed, but from Jonathan's contribution, it all seemed to center around his various business interests that had been launched since he had been in Green Pond and what would be required to make a number of fund transfers between the various entities quickly. Chloe's knowledge of the details of such subjects was limited, to say the least, but even so, she was sure that was the subject of the call. It was certainly a stretch at that point, but Chloe soon began to interpret the overall picture that Jonathan possibly wanted to liquidate a large amount of his invested capital. *Is he preparing for a sudden and unannounced departure from Green Pond? Was he, in fact, the one behind Teresa's murder —either by his own hand or a hired gun—and now planning to flee and go into hiding?*

Those were the questions that came to Chloe's mind right away, but she caught herself before her imagination went completely off the rails. First of all, if he had been behind her murder, then why wait three years to go on the run? Unless he needed to wait for some of his investments to begin to turn a profit to allow him the cash he thought he might need to go underground. Also, if he did indeed love Adam and Katie as much as everyone claimed, then she could not see him abandoning them. However, taking them with him might open up a whole can of worms that he did not want hanging over his head if he were the murderer. How do you explain that to two kids as bright and perceptive as Adam and Katie?

But maybe the belief in town over his culpability is gaining strength, even in the light of a possible police payoff. Maybe something new in the way of physical evidence has surfaced that she and Harold have no knowledge of? If those two items were at play, maybe Jonathan felt he could no longer wait and just continue clinging to his alibi. It would explain the three-year wait, anyway. She dared a quick peek through the gap and saw Jonathan madly scribbling notes on a pad as if whoever were on the other end of the call—maybe an accountant or other financial advisor of some ilk—was giving him exactly what he needed to know to rearrange his finances.

But even so, if this is true, what can she do? I mean, she told herself, all she had was some idle talk from town plus a partially overheard phone conversation. It did not look good from her perspective at the moment, but then again, maybe not hearing the whole call was making her jump to conclusions. After all, her background in finance was slim to none. A sudden gust of wind sprung up and made some stems from bushes next to the mansion scrape unexpectedly against the window inside the office. It made Jonathan look up quickly as if he thought maybe someone had seen him, and Chloe clamped her hand over her mouth to prevent a gasp from escaping, as the sudden noise caught her off guard as well.

She snapped her head back just as Jonathan took a careful look backward, and her heart began to pound wildly as she knew she had just managed to avoid being spotted. She froze in place, too petrified to move a muscle that might give him a reason to check where she was standing just then. Chloe knew it had just been some random wind and that it made no sense for him to come looking, but knowing her eavesdropping was really wrong, she pressed into the corridor wall anyway. A few tense seconds ticked by, and Chloe did not relax until she heard Jonathan go back to his call.

"Sorry, Andy," Jonathan said, "I thought I heard something here, but it was just the wind."

Chloe exhaled as silently as possible and knew she had pushed her luck as far as she should.

"So, is that all that we need to do?" Jonathan asked, going back to his conversation.

A few beats went by as all he did was say "okay" and "hmm" a few times.

"Good enough, Andy. Let me do a few calculations on my own, and I'll get back to you."

Chloe panicked as she realized the call was ending sooner than she had anticipated. What did she do now? Moving ahead to the kitchen might raise his suspicions that she had heard everything but rushing back upstairs might make too much of a racket. With only a few seconds to make a decision, Chloe opted for some-where between those two choices. She pushed off the wall and carefully stepped backward toward the stair-case, hoping to just be coming down the hallway as

Jonathan exited his office. Then she could just say she had come down for a glass of water.

Her plan seemed to be working perfectly until one wayward step back caused an old floorboard in the hallway to groan and creak over the complete stillness of the quiet mansion. Chloe froze as Jonathan rushed to the door and looked right at her. Chloe knew she was screwed.

27

MAY 2008

*I*t had been ages since Chloe had been in a position where she felt like she had been caught red-handed at something she had no business being involved in. Actually, she thought, it had not been since she was a freshman in college, and she and some friends had gotten caught trying to sneak back into their dorm well beyond the hours set for week-days. At the time, it had seemed horrific to her as a naïve eighteen-year-old who had never broken the rules in her parent's home. But later, her friends assured her it was no big deal. They would just have to toe the line the rest of the year to avoid being written up officially. And so it had been...

But right now, as she stood in the hallway, frozen like a deer caught in a car's headlights, Chloe briefly felt taken back to that day when she was just eighteen again. But a lot of water had flowed under the bridge for her since those days, and Chloe knew she could talk her way out of this potential minefield, at least she hoped she could, as the look on Jonathan's face just now was not good.

"Jonathan!" Chloe exclaimed, feigning surprise as she dramatically clasped her hands to her chest as if he had scared her to death. "You startled me. I thought you were off to Boston?"

Chloe had often heard the old sports adage that the best defense was a good offense, and she hoped she was pulling that off. His expression was a mixture of the same coldness that he had always shown her overlaid with a slight tinge of suspicion, and Chloe wondered if he had somehow known how long she had been in the hallway.

"It got canceled at the last minute and rescheduled for tomorrow in California. What are you doing up so late?"

His blunt and annoyed tone gave her pause, but then again, most of that was just how he had always been with them ever since they had arrived. Chloe brushed off her anxiety and plowed ahead.

"Oh…just couldn't sleep. I guess the new space and all and all the things racing through my brain that I want to use to help Adam and Katie and all. Sometimes it just takes me a few days to get comfortable in an unfamiliar place. I thought maybe a glass of warm milk might help me sleep."

He did not reply right away, and for just a moment, Chloe was sure that somehow he knew she had heard at least some of his conversation. He just looked at her and frowned.

"I see. Sorry if I spooked you. I just had to grab

some papers and files to take with me. Everything else okay?"

"Perfect! The kids and I are getting on wonderfully!"

Jonathan just nodded without saying anything more, which was partly a relief to Chloe though she could not ignore the hard gaze in his eyes that he was unsure if he really believed her. He bid her good night and left the mansion through the front door. Chloe sighed heavily and leaned against the wall as her legs trembled from the interaction. She was beginning to recover just as she heard Jonathan drive off, and she went to one of the long, narrow windows that sat on either side of the front door just to make sure. With the episode over, Chloe did, in fact, proceed to the kitchen to get some water as her mouth was dry as sand.

As she washed out the glass and put it in the draining rack, she looked out over the cleared property to the west. It was a clear and cloudless night, and the moon made the grounds look like something out of a picture postcard.

"I got news for you, pal," Chloe said softly to herself as she pondered her interaction with Jonathan, "you are not the only one who was spinning a tale tonight."

It was not much, she realized, but after all that had just happened, Chloe was now becoming a growing believer that Ralph Yardley and his cronies might be onto something. She would keep thinking it over and maybe even seeing if she could dig up anything more in support of it, but at the moment, Chloe was pretty damn sure that Jonathan Thompson had had some hand in Teresa's murder. Whether it was for financial gain—very unlikely she figured—or for some personal interest—more likely—she did not know. But everything about Jonathan now screamed potential murderer to her.

28

JUNE 2008

A few days later, May's clear and sunny weather turned overcast and heavy clouds brought some much-needed, but not especially well-timed, rain to Green Pond. The farmers were grateful as May had been especially dry, and if that was to be a preview of what was to come for the summer growing months, then they were in big trouble. But for Tony and Harold and his guys at the mansion, it was yet one more obstacle for them to work around. After getting the roof patched in spots that had needed it for a very long time, Tony had big plans for an overhaul in the facings around the entire roofline plus touching up all the neglected seals everywhere that would set up a situation for numerable leaks if a really heavy storm came their way. Green Pond was close enough to the coast that tropical disturbances that blew up the Atlantic shoreline were a major concern.

But as the week began in which he had planned to have the entire team tackle that chore, he saw it would have to be put off until the weather cleared. Not only was the pitch of the roof too dangerous to work on when it was wet, but none of the sealants and adhesives he needed to use would have time to cure in the damp weather. It was not a catastrophe, seeing as how there was still plenty of other projects for them to address on the interior, but just one more change in his schedule that made his contract with Jonathan remain in constant flux. On this occasion, though, some basic prep work needed to get done in the cellar and then up in the attic before he could have Harold join him to do the fine finishing work, so he told Harold to just take a day or two off and relax until his guys had their part of the interior work completed.

Harold was actually thankful for the time off as he had strained a spot in his lower back that had given him trouble on and off for years, and it was a perfect time for him to let it heal a bit. But that did not mean that he had any intention of just sitting around and putting his feet up completely. He and Chloe had talked at length after her recent interaction with Jonathan, and he felt that Chloe was definitely onto a possibility that there was way more to the grieving Jonathan Thompson than met the eye. The local gossip from town was one thing, and Danny's perhaps skewed opinion of him another, but what they needed, they decided, was some real objective evidence from some other source maybe not so close to the man himself.

"Ralph Yardley and his pals in Green Pond might actually have some ulterior motive in pointing a finger Jonathan's way in regard to Teresa's killer," Harold said as they sat in the solarium, sipping coffee as the temperatures outside fell off and a gentle, but growing rainstorm began, pattering the glass with a pleasant rhythm.

"You mean like jealousy over his wealth, or maybe he rubbed someone the wrong way once upon a time… maybe over some business in town or something?" Chloe asked.

"Precisely, and I think Danny's so devoted and protective of his brother that his view might be a bit biased as well. I'm not saying it's not true, but if Jonathan did pull this off, then maybe Danny was just as in the dark about it as everyone else."

"Seeing him through the rose-colored glasses of their youth?"

"Could be…I mean, he did say they had fallen out of touch. Maybe Danny is just going overboard to try to make amends for his guilt over that."

Chloe nodded and sipped her coffee as a far-off rumble of thunder echoed through the forest. "So, who do we talk to who might not have an agenda?"

"Actually, I've been giving that some thought ever since you told me about what you overheard that night in Jonathan's office."

"And?"

"How about Reggie Foster?"

Chloe raised her eyebrows inquiringly. "He hadn't occurred to me, but he might be the perfect person to chat with and get a view of the Thompson family that both true outsiders and close family would not have."

29

JUNE 2008

*I*n just the few weeks they had been at Aberdeen Estates, Harold and Chloe had developed a nice, congenial relationship with the talented and affable chef. Reggie was one of those guys you could feel you had known forever after just meeting him based on his open and accepting personality and folksy charm. As they already knew, Reggie had his roots in Baton Rouge and had come to be the personal chef for Jonathan Thompson years ago, stepping in to relieve Teresa of some of that responsibility so she could focus on Adam and Katie. He had been a bit cagey when it came to just how it was that he had landed at Aberdeen Estates, but Harold and Chloe both felt that was probably more of an issue with something that had happened on his route to get there or possibly some family turmoil or tragedy than anything to do with Thompson himself.

"He's been here long enough to have a pretty good idea of the real dynamic of the family, I think," Harold said. "With his skills and personality, I'm guessing Reggie could write his own ticket. Must be something here that has held him in place for so long."

"From what he earned in his former career, I bet Jonathan is paying him pretty well. That could be one thing. But maybe there was something else in Green Pond that made Reggie decide this was home."

"A girl?"

Chloe grinned and shrugged. "Always a possibility, I guess, but I was thinking maybe just something about Green Pond that made him feel at home and welcome."

"And if that's the case, he might be the ideal person to show us a more realistic picture of what might have been going on inside the walls here—like what kind of man Jonathan really is, what his relationship with Teresa was really like…that kind of thing."

"Good point. And if he is being paid well—which I am sure he is—then there is no real jealousy aspect in regard to Jonathan's money that might exist for some of the townies. Plus, there is no family connection to color his opinion like Danny may be operating under."

"And more importantly, a question we have yet to hear the answer to except for just sheer gossip and idle talk. Was there anything going on that might have made it seem like Jonathan might want his wife out of the picture?"

Chloe nodded eagerly.

"But we just need to approach him in a casual manner and without it looking as if we're grilling him for information. The last thing we want to do is make him feel like we're pointing a finger at his boss and causing waves that might disrupt his very comfortable way of making a living here."

* * *

THE NEXT MORNING the weather continued to stay just as it had for the better part of the week, and no one seemed in a hurry to leave the wonderful aromas and warm temperatures filling the kitchen. Knowing that Harold was nursing a sore back and taking some time away from his work with Tony, Reggie prepared a more extensive offering that morning and then joined them at the table with a large mug of his rich coffee while they ate. Harold and Chloe saw that as the perfect time to chat the chef up about Casa de Thompson, and Chloe sent Adam and Katie off to their room with some homework to keep them occupied while they talked to Reggie.

"Man, this coffee is killer, Reggie!" Harold exclaimed as they sat and enjoyed the slower pace of the day. "What's in here that makes it so special? I've never tasted anything like it."

"Aside from the special blend I found that I order from Costa Rica, I've done some experimenting over time. Just trying this and that, but I think what you're tasting is chicory."

"Sure," Chloe replied, "I've heard of that. But that can't be all. There's something else here I'm picking up. I just can't put my finger on it."

Reggie put down his mug and just smiled but said nothing.

"You're staying mum on that?" Harold asked with a grin.

"Like a great magician, if you knew what went on behind the curtain, then you wouldn't think it was magic."

"Like one of those things you hear in those cheesy spy movies that if you told us, you'd have to kill us?" Chloe said with a chuckle.

"Something like that," Reggie replied, and they all laughed.

Harold shot Chloe a sly glance, indicating that might be a good time to ask some questions seeing as how they might just be seen as part of a casual conversation and not an interrogation. She nodded so as not to let Reggie see.

"So you've been here ever since Jonathan and Teresa bought the mansion?" Chloe asked.

"Not quite...about a year or so after when she needed help with meals. Jonathan felt the kids were consuming more and more of her time as they got older, and he wanted to give her a break."

"Did she mind having you take over her kitchen?"

Reggie threw back his head and howled. "Teresa Thompson? Hardly...lovely woman but a spatula and a whisk were not her best friends, if you get my meaning."

Harold and Chloe laughed with him.

"No, I think she was more relieved than insulted, though I understand your question. Most women I know are pretty protective of their kitchens."

They chatted around the main event for a few more

minutes before Chloe launched into what they really wanted to get from him.

"Were you here the night she got killed?" Chloe asked.

Reggie grimaced a bit.

"Oh, jeez, I'm sorry, Reggie. It's okay if you don't want to relive that."

"Nah…it's okay. It just brings back a lot of bad memories, is all. Yeah, I was here. I mean not here, here, but I was around. Found out about it the next morning like everyone else when the police and the ambulance arrived."

"And still a mystery after all this time," Harold added.

"Yeah…very sad."

"Harold ran into this guy in town who has this theory that Jonathan was somehow involved but that the police just didn't pursue that. You know about that?"

Reggie sighed and looked away. "Yeah, I've heard all that. Ralph Yardley and his bunch. Everyone is entitled to an opinion, but I wouldn't give a whole lot of weight to anything old Ralph has to say on any subject."

"Oh?" Harold asked.

"He means well, I think, but Ralph sees conspiracies around every corner and in every crack of the walls. Ask him about the 1969 moon landing one day, and you'll see what I mean."

"Yikes," Chloe replied to keep the conversation moving.

"As far as my knowledge of what went on that

night, I have no idea. I know for a fact that Jonathan was away, but other than that, it's just as baffling to me now as it was three years ago."

"You said Teresa was a lovely woman," Chloe pressed.

"That she was. She treated me like one of the family."

"Was that the overall opinion of Teresa Thompson around town then?" Harold added.

"I'd say that's accurate, at least as far as I know. It's not like there's anyone in Green Pond I know of that was anything but shocked and appalled by her murder.

"And when Jonathan did find out, it was like all the air just went out of him. I think he was devastated for Adam and Katie, knowing they had actually found her body before the police arrived. Nothing means more in this world to him than those kids."

Harold nodded as he looked toward Chloe. He was not sure if she had picked up on it or not, but Reggie had said nothing about how her actual death had impacted Jonathan. He just spoke of it in terms of how it had affected the children. Maybe it was just his inter-pretation and a minor discrepancy in how it had been framed, but he knew that with or without children that if anything like that should ever happen to Chloe, he would be emotionally dead. The night before, they had discussed whether or not to directly address the reports they had come across of a relationship between Jonathan and Teresa that included a bit more than just minor disagreements and spats common to any marriage.

Harold had said he would let her take the lead on that topic when and if the time seemed right, and he was hoping she saw this break as the time. Chloe did not disappoint him.

"We had heard that she and Jonathan argued and fought from time to time. You ever around when any of that was going on?" she asked.

Reggie hesitated before speaking. "I feel awkward talking behind Jonathan's back about that and all, but I'm sure the investigators considered that piece. And with her dead now these three years and Jonathan not possibly being responsible, I guess there's no harm in telling you."

"So there was some conflict?" Harold added.

Reggie nodded sheepishly. "Yeah…on and off. And sometimes it got pretty nasty."

Harold and Chloe perked up as that was the first time they had had anyone actually suggest that the apparent perfect little lives of Jonathan and Teresa Thompson might not have been so innocent.

30

JUNE 2008

*R*eggie refilled their mugs and then sat down again, still looking a bit as if he was somewhat uncomfortable revealing what had gone on behind closed doors at Aberdeen Estates during his employment. "Initially, it was just the normal arguments or differences of opinion that you might expect between any married couple, I guess. I've never been married, so I'm just assuming here. You know…maybe a raised voice or two or words spoken out of emotion or circumstances that might have been regretted later."

Harold and Chloe nodded and smirked. That was not a common event in their own lives, but they had to admit it had not been unknown back in Hampton.

"Anyway, calmer minds normally prevailed, and it wasn't like these were long-standing grudges or times where one or the other refused to back down or forgive the other later on."

"Something tells me that was not always the case, though," Chloe said quietly.

Reggie nodded regretfully and went on. "Yeah. Sadly, once Jonathan announced that he wanted to get back into a more professional life than he had planned on when they had left New York for Green Pond, a different atmosphere set in."

"Teresa was not too keen on this plan?" Harold asked.

"I don't think it was the idea itself that she was opposed to, but that from his description, he was going to be away from home way more than she was comfortable with. New place and being left with all the responsibilities of the house...like that."

"But we were told she said this was fine when it happened," Chloe replied.

"Yeah, that was the outer layer. Teresa knew Jonathan was growing bored with the slow pace of life here after they had lived in New York. He had underestimated adjusting to leaving his business behind."

"How did you find this out?" Harold asked.

"Oh, as you can imagine, Teresa didn't have a ton of friends here, being so new to the town, so a lot of times when I was puttering around in the kitchen, she would drop by. We would just talk. I think she just needed someone to listen to her concerns."

"Was she angry?" Chloe asked.

"No, not really...more just frustrated and confused, I think. I don't know this for sure, but I got the feeling she had a much different vision of their new life in Green Pond than what seemed to be happening all of a sudden."

"And it was the frequent travel that bothered her most?" Chloe asked.

"I would say so from what we talked about. Tony was always around to help out when he could, but he had his hands full with the renovation. I think Teresa was a bit hesitant to bug him unless it was a real emergency. She wanted to put up this brave front for everyone and support Jonathan as best she could even though she didn't like it too much."

"Was she concerned that he might be seeing other women on the road?" Chloe continued.

"No, nothing like that...just that she felt she was shouldering everything in Green Pond. Their relationship might have been strained by this time, but not due to any suspicions of an affair...never."

"So you became her sounding board?" Harold asked.

"I did. And like Tony, I was available to help if I could."

"But she didn't ask much, huh?" Chloe added.

"Other than my normal duties in the kitchen and just being around to hear her out, that was about it."

"This is a touchy question, Reggie, and if it's too personal, just say so," Harold said.

He nodded for him to go on.

"Did you ever encourage her to have a more serious discussion with Jonathan about how she really felt?"

Reggie sighed again and took a long sip from his mug. "When we sat and talked at length, all I had to draw on for advice to her was from how I grew up back in Baton Rouge. My family was pretty communicative with one another, and for me, if there was something on your mind, you just sat down and hashed it out. So, yeah, that was my advice to her. That she sit with him and really make her feelings known before they ate her up inside or there was just some emotional explosion from trying to hold it all in…maybe sparked by some minor, unrelated incident."

"I'm guessing she took your advice," Harold commented.

"That she did, and to this day, I'm not sure if that was the best advice I could have offered at the time. I mean, just because that was my experience doesn't mean it was the best for everyone. As you might have noticed, Jonathan is not the warmest and emotionally available person on the planet."

"That's not your fault, Reggie," Chloe said quickly. "You offered your best advice at the time, and it was her decision to act on it. I mean, she probably knew Jonathan as a person better than anyone and how he might take a direct confrontation."

"I know, I know, but I still feel some responsibility for what happened next and that maybe things might have been different for them if I'd really thought out what I said to her."

"You said early on that things sometimes got nasty. Was that after Teresa made her true feelings known?" Chloe asked.

Reggie just nodded. "Things just kind of snowballed after that, I guess. You could see how uncomfortable Jonathan was when she finally bared her soul about how she really felt, but by then, it was too late to go back. From what I overheard, Teresa was very respectful and tactful in her feelings, but Jonathan took it the wrong way, in my opinion, and interpreted it as an attack on him personally. Like all that he provided for her was not enough and that she was trying to deny him this new opportunity that he wanted to pursue out of her own self-interest."

"Uh-oh," Harold interjected.

"Yeah, anyway, things turned frosty between them for a bit before the real fireworks started. Jonathan was bored in Green Pond and wanted to have this thing in his life to alleviate his ennui. He tried to frame it as being for the family's future, but Teresa knew as well as anyone that they had enough money to last over many lifetimes. To her, it was never about the family's security. For Teresa, it was just Jonathan's own inner drive and ego that seemed to have no end to what they wanted."

"And this went on until the day she was killed?" Harold asked.

Reggie nodded and grimaced. "When he was in town, the fights and arguments got quite heated and lengthy, like neither one of them could let go of their position. He had not yet arrived back in the States, but still, Danny tried to intervene from abroad when word got back to him about how volatile and unsettled everything was becoming here. Like all of us, we were concerned about how this vitriol and animosity affected Adam and Katie. Although I think Danny was already planning to come back, I'm pretty sure that sped up his timetable for that decision."

They all just sat for a few seconds and said nothing.

"And you mentioned this to the police during their investigation?" Harold finally asked.

"I did but seeing as how he was out of town when Teresa was murdered, they didn't see any of it as relevant to her death."

Chloe was still not convinced that if Jonathan were angry enough at Teresa, he might have gone mad—even temporarily—and paid someone to take care of her. But that seemed way too accusatory to suggest to Reggie, seeing as how he had been so kind and forthcoming with all this background they were unaware of.

31

JUNE 2008

*R*eggie collected all the dirty mugs and went to the sink to clean up. As he worked there, Chloe decided to float one last thing by him just because she was curious based on her own beliefs and what Adam and Katie had claimed to have seen recently.

"Say, Reggie," she began, "have you ever seen or heard anything weird here that didn't seem to have any rational or logical explanation?"

"Like what?"

"Well, we got this story from some locals about this old legend they call the Aberdeen ghost. Supposedly, the wife of the man who built this place is said to haunt the halls and rooms here."

He chuckled as he put the last mug in the draining rack. "Oh, yeah, I've heard that from time to time since I've been here, but I can't say I have ever seen or heard anything that would convince me it has any merit."

"Do you believe in that stuff?"

"I don't know. I guess anything is possible, but it's not like I'm a confirmed believer or denier one way or the other. All I'm aware of here are just the odd creaks and groans of an old house that is still settling over time. Nothing that I would say is supernatural or paranormal. Plus, there's so much renovation going on now that a lot of the noise that filters down to me is probably just Tony and his guys, I always figured. Why?"

Chloe hesitated but knew she was the one who had started this conversation. "Well, the kids tell me they have seen a vision of their mother in the mansion."

"Really?"

"So they say. She never speaks to them or touches them but just drops by like she's making sure they're all right."

"You believe them, Chloe?"

"I believe they saw something. Whether or not it's real or just their imaginations as part of how they're coping with the loss, I can't say."

"I'm typically gone as soon as dinner is over anyway. I've never stayed here overnight when things are quieter, so who knows for sure. Neither Adam nor Katie ever said anything about that to me, but I would vote for the latter. Kids their age typically have wild imaginations, you know?"

Chloe just nodded and did not reply to that as she was not so sure. Both she and Harold figured they had pushed Reggie about as far as they could without making him more suspicious about their curiosity than he might already be. They thanked him for breakfast and the talk and headed off to what had once been an old library in the original mansion to discuss the new information and what it all meant when taken with what they already knew.

* * *

THEY SAT in overstuffed easy chairs and threw ideas back and forth regarding what they should do next, if anything. Though finding out more about what went on behind the doors at the mansion had been eye-opening, it seemed to feel like it just presented more questions regarding the truth behind Teresa's murder than it offered an answer.

"As I see it," Harold began, "we've got a couple options here. One, we just resign this gig and get our asses back to Hampton and try to pick up the pieces of what we left behind. I'd hate to have those kids walked out on again, and it bugs me professionally to walk away from a promise I made to Tony."

"I agree completely. That's an option, but I have this feeling it'll bother me in the days to come if we do that."

"Okay. I only bring that up in case our poking around might get back to the wrong person and put us in harm's way."

"Like if the real killer is still hanging around Green Pond?"

Harold nodded.

"What else?" Chloe asked.

"Okay, number two. Just ignore all that we've come across and keep plugging away at our respective jobs until those obligations to Jonathan have been fulfilled."

"That one really sucks, Harold," Chloe replied as she waved it away.

"Yeah, I know, but I'm just trying to consider all options at this point. I can't see either of us just going through the motions as if nothing has changed. I don't know about you, but that would make me nuts."

Chloe nodded her agreement. "Any more?" she asked.

"Well, there's one more which I am sure you have already considered. It is, to me anyway, the most rational of the three, but also perhaps the most dangerous and risky."

"Talk to Jonathan?" Chloe asked.

Harold nodded and continued, "Yep. Go to him directly and confront him with what we have heard that made us curious about our situation here. Let him defend the stories and then decide what's next for us."

Chloe exhaled in nervousness. "I know it's probably the most rational, but what if Jonathan *is* the murderer or hired one?"

"Yeah, I know. That's the fly in the ointment picking that one. Doesn't leave us much in the way of protection if that's the case."

Chloe just nodded and appeared to be mulling over all that Harold had offered. "You think that maybe the stress of what we just went through in Hampton and now being in this new place with this, shall we say, interesting back history, is coloring our perceptions?"

"Could be. I hadn't considered that, actually."

"Okay, here's the thing, Harold. I love those kids, and like everyone else here, I'm really concerned about their welfare going forward. I don't want to be just another nanny who cuts and runs at the first sign of trouble."

"I know. And the commitment I made to Tony through Jonathan is one I would do anything to keep. Not so much for Jonathan himself, I guess, but it's really not fair to leave Tony holding the bag...again."

"Despite the risk, I feel the last option is our only reasonable choice."

"Me, too. Before we would go to anyone in any official capacity, I think we need to give Jonathan the chance to lay out his side of the story in case the talk from town is just that and nothing more. It's hard to just take a few people's opinions as fact when there may be serious personal agendas at work behind it all."

"How about we sleep on this before making any final decisions one way or the other. Also, we need to come up with an approach to Jonathan that will not make him feel like he is being put on the defensive—even though he actually will be—and maybe backed into a corner that he can't escape from intact. He's not due back here for a day or two anyway."

"Good idea. How about a quick drink, and then we turn in?"

They downed a quick brandy and then headed up the hallway toward the staircase, dowsing the lights as they went, hoping a good night's sleep would present them a solid game plan for approaching Jonathan upon his return to Green Pond, assuming they both still felt like that was the way to go. But just as they stepped onto the first step, they both froze and stared in disbelief and wonder at what lay just ahead of them about halfway down the flight.

32

JUNE 2008

*H*overing over the wide expanse of the staircase, they stood and gaped at this glowing and pulsating orb of white mist that slowly began to condense and take the form of a woman. She looked upon them with a steely gaze, not really seeming to indicate any aggression or other danger but definitely letting them know she was a presence to be reckoned with. Even in her final form, there was no way around her, even if Harold or Chloe had considered that seemingly foolhardy thought. She held her arms wide as if receiving something from the air around her until her features, though not crystal-clear, began to take a more defined appearance.

She was not a large person, but there was just something in her countenance that gave them pause all the same. Chloe touched Harold on the arm lightly as it hit her as to just who this was…Teresa Thompson. She had seen enough photos from all the press coverage of her murder and the subsequent investigation to recognize her despite her somewhat amorphous and gauzy appearance now.

"Teresa?" Harold asked quietly.

Chloe just nodded.

"Any idea what she might want or why she's appearing to us now?"

"Who do I look like, The Amazing Kreskin?" she replied in a whisper.

The Teresa apparition did not move any closer toward them, nor did she utter any words or any other kind of vocalization. She just looked at them with a steady, unflinching stare, her golden hair blowing back from her head in a wind that apparently only affected her. She did not frown or scowl at them, but neither did she smile. All that was on her face was a look of grim seriousness that gave off the message that she was not moving away anytime soon.

"What now?" Harold asked.

"Beats me," Chloe replied as she felt her heart pound away.

Though she had been through a ghostly experience in her past, Chloe was still unnerved and unsure about what the hell Teresa wanted and what to do next. In her experience in that cavern back in Virginia when she was just a kid, the apparition had never actually seen her...as far as she knew anyway. It had just materialized and then passed along in its search in the twisting tunnels of the old caves. This time she felt somewhat immobilized, curiously unable to move forward or backward as the specter held them with an overpowering stare.

"Should we speak to her?" Harold whispered into Chloe's ear.

"Just a guess, but I don't think that would do any good right now."

"You getting any feeling that she means us harm, or is it something else? This is beginning to feel like the old hackneyed Mexican standoff if you get my meaning."

Chloe nodded slightly. "I don't get the sense that she's dangerous to us. I'm just winging it here, but my gut tells me she just wants us to know that she's for real and not some imaginary creation out of the minds of Adam and Katie."

Harold exhaled gently to try to shed off the anxiety building inside him. This type of thing was his first live encounter with anything paranormal, and it was simultaneously fascinating and unsettling. His fading skepticism at such things was now completely gone, and he was totally on board with Chloe at that moment that such things were, in fact, real. It is not that he had ever doubted her belief in all of it, but more that he just needed to see it first-hand. He supposed it was just how he was.

"This how it was for you when you were a kid and saw whatever it was in that cavern you told me about?"

"Nope. That entity never saw me—I don't think—but this just feels completely different from that. Back then, this palpable emotion of great sorrow and desperation seemed to come over me as that apparition passed by me. With this, well, it is hard to say, but if I had to make a prediction, I would say Teresa has an agenda for us."

"Oh, shit…"

"But I don't get the sense that it puts us in harm's way. Both Adam and Katie had said she just deemed to drop by to make sure they were doing well, not to talk to them. I'm wondering if this manifestation is just to make us aware of her as a real entity. Maybe she felt that needed to be established before her next step in her plan."

"Next step?"

Chloe shrugged. "I don't know, but if the kids were her whole world, then maybe, just maybe, Teresa is thinking of recruiting us to help solve her murder? I mean, besides the killer, she's the only one who really knows the truth."

Harold thought that over, and though it was hard to wrap his mind around this new way of thinking, it made sense on some level.

"You thinking she'll eventually just vanish and then come back again later with…I don't know…instructions or other information to get our help?"

"Who knows? That's just a feeling I get right now. I figure if she meant us harm, she would have done so by now. And besides, what would be accomplished by hurting us anyway?"

Harold had to agree that her logic made sense. If you could actually apply logic to a situation like this, that was. He touched Chloe on the sleeve and indicated they should sit and wait this out. He did not know why, but everything Chloe had said to him had convinced him she was right on target with her theory. Maybe showing Teresa they were not afraid and saw her as a benevolent entity would help. Chloe got his unspoken message and then slowly sank to the bottom step, never taking their eyes away from Teresa so she would not get the impression they were dismissing her.

Suddenly a thin smile began to form on her face, and she bent her elbows, bringing her palms together in front of her chest in a gesture of thanks. The previous atmosphere Harold and Chloe had felt of being held against their will, to some degree, lifted, and the house felt as it always had before Teresa had come to them.

"You suppose she knows we get it?" Harold asked.

"Could be. Maybe her abilities and perceptions are so different in her state now that actual spoken words are not needed?"

"Like telepathy or something?"

Chloe shrugged, but in her heart, she felt that was true. So they sat and looked up as the now benevolent-looking Teresa-thing smiled at them and seemed to radiate a feeling of appreciation and warmth. The seconds ticked by slowly as all still seemed to be in a holding pattern until Teresa's defined form began to waver slightly and lose its human form. The white hue began to change little by little into a mixture of blue and violet, and Chloe grasped Harold firmly by the arm, a pang of fear in her stomach, as the smile began to drop away from Teresa's face and a pained grimace took over. It seemed impossible that a ghostly entity could experience anything as mundane as physical pain or discomfort from this world, but Chloe supposed anything was possible. In the depths of her mind, she wondered if she had been way off in her supposition and that the situation was about to take a decidedly negative turn for them.

33

JUNE 2008

The dissolution of Teresa's image continued to become greater and greater as they looked on with growing concern as she seemed to just be imploding on herself, though what was left of her expression still looked quite pained and distressed. Slowly, the amorphous ball of mist replaced her detailed form, but it retained this new blue-violet tint as it hung in the air before them. Chloe felt her pulse heighten as the unknown of what was transpiring filled her with trepidation. But then, just as calmly and as simply as the original fog had appeared to them earlier, the mist fell in on itself to a tight dense ball which then just dissolved away, bit by bit, until Harold and Chloe found themselves staring at an empty staircase again.

They looked at each other briefly, neither quite sure of what had just happened.

"Well, there's something you don't see every day," Harold said as he finally relaxed.

"For sure. I've never seen anything quite like that,

even back when I was a kid in that cavern," Chloe replied as she felt her heart beginning to slow.

"What do you suppose that sudden change in her facial expression was?"

"Who knows? It looked to me like she never felt any discomfort until it was time for her to go back to wherever it was she exists now."

"Like the process of manifesting involved some…I don't know…pain or stress?"

"I suppose. I never would have imagined that the transformation in and out of her current location would expose her to such a thing, but that makes as much sense as anything to me."

"Maybe it just takes an extra drain of energy or something to make the jump."

Chloe shrugged. "In any case, I guess we can pretty much figure out what that was all about, huh?"

"It would seem so. Teresa Thompson is no imaginary creation out of the minds of those kids, and I would be shocked if there's not more to come."

"So does that mean you're putting the lingering threads of your skepticism over the paranormal and supernatural to bed for once and all?"

"What other explanation is there, Chloe? Before, I was certainly still on the fence about it all, but now, well, it sounds silly, but I guess, seeing is believing."

"True. I'm still shaking a bit."

"So, do we just wait for her to appear again and maybe point us in the correct direction if, in fact, she's trying to enlist us to bring her killer to justice after all this time?"

"I'm not sure if that's our best next step or if we need to be more proactive, you know? This is just too incredible and stunning to make a snap decision, though. How about we head up to bed to see if we can figure this out tomorrow when it might all make more sense?"

Harold nodded, flipped on the light that illuminated the top of the stairs, and they both plodded up, still feeling drained and spent from Teresa's appearance. They moved down the hall and went to their room after peeking in quickly to check on Adam and Katie.

HAROLD AND CHLOE TURNED IN, but neither could settle down enough to sleep following what they had just seen on top of everything else. Chloe lay flat on her back and tried to meditate her way to sleep. But if the analogy that many practitioners of the technique used to describe an overactive feeling of "monkey mind" was accurate, then Chloe figured King Kong had found his way off the Empire State Building and into her subconscious. She tossed and turned and finally decided to get up so she didn't wake Harold. But unbeknownst to her, he was no closer to nodding off than she was, and he sat up when she swung her feet to the floor on her side of the bed.

"I'm sorry, Harold. Did I wake you?"

"No chance. I gave all those practices you normally talk about when you are having some infrequent bouts of insomnia, but either I'm lousy at the techniques, or this is all just too much to push away at the moment."

"I'm guessing it has nothing to do with your efforts. Maybe we should try to talk this out a bit since sleep seems like it's not an option."

They both sat back against the headboard and used just the small bedside table lamp beside Chloe to light the room.

Harold sighed and took her hand. "Wonder if maybe we are in over our heads here, Chloe?"

"You having second thoughts about going straight to Jonathan when he gets back?"

"Yeah. I think I am. Before tonight, I guess I thought it might be worth a shot, but now…I'm not so sure. I mean, if Jonathan did kill Teresa, and her coming to us tonight might indicate that, though I'm just guessing here, then that would put us right in his crosshairs."

"Same thing occurred to me. Right now, I don't see anyone else—unless you want to try to tag this thing on some random homicide from a stranger who broke in —who's a likely candidate."

"You mean like Teresa surprised some intruder and was just in the wrong place at the wrong time?"

Chloe nodded. "But that just doesn't feel right to me."

"Me either."

"I guess the great unknown is still whether or not Jonathan lied about being out of town and snuck back here to do the deed himself or hired someone."

"As well as what his driving motive would be. I mean, it seems way over the top to me to kill your wife based on some arguments, no matter how heated or volatile they had become."

"Or there's some underlying reason we're totally unaware of. Right now, it's all just guesswork."

They sat silently for a few moments as a light and steady sprinkle of rain pattered on the windowpane.

"I don't know, Chloe. Despite all the reasons we both want to fulfill our promises and obligations here to Jonathan, I'm not sure it's worth risking our lives over it if what we suspect is true."

"Yeah, I would hate myself for just up and taking off, but I agree that it's minor considering it might be in return for our very lives."

"How about this? Rather than look unprofessional and uncaring, how about we leave a message with Danny and explain the situation...not all of it, obviously, but that...let's say...maybe framing it like we're having experiences here that make us wary about staying on or that circumstances have arisen for us that we didn't anticipate when we accepted the gig. Something like that."

"Touch on the legend, maybe?"

"I know he's not so keen on that story or anything paranormal for that matter, but I guess it's worth a try. Remember he said we could come to him any time if we had any problems. That way, we would not be putting ourselves in any real potential danger with Jonathan if this is all true. At this point, I think Danny might be our only safe out."

Chloe thought that over, and it made sense. She still did not like leaving Adam and Katie in a lurch, but after what she and Harold had been through in Hampton, she knew she needed to take care of herself first.

"Okay...it's almost 5 AM now. Let's call Danny, and hopefully, his voicemail will pick up, and we won't throw him into a panic like it was in the middle of the night."

Harold nodded, and he dialed the number Danny Thompson had left them and sighed with relief when the recording for his voicemail kicked in. He left the message that he and Chloe had carefully crafted. Then they began to gather their stuff together so they could head back to Hampton as soon as there was another adult on the property to take care of the children. The rain picked up a touch as they hurriedly packed. An ominous echo of thunder rambled toward them, making Harold sure they were making the correct decision. However, he was certain he was just letting his perception of a normal summer storm color his logic. Regardless, he just could not justify putting them in a potentially lethal situation to fulfill a promise made on an oral agreement and handshake.

By the time they finally had gotten their things stowed away and were heading out, the rain had stopped and the sun was just seeping through the gaps in the eastern-facing trees as the rain from earlier dripped from the saturated foliage. But as Harold was tossing their last bag into the trunk, he looked up to see Danny's car racing toward them up the slight incline of the gravel drive. He slid to a sudden stop, threw open his door, and rushed toward them without bothering to close the driver's door of his car or even turn off the engine.

Harold waited on him as the look on Danny's face was one of desperation and worry. Chloe glanced over from her spot in the passenger's seat, wondering how bad this was going to be. But if she had seen Danny from Harold's perspective, she would have instantly known that he was not angry, just incredibly distraught.

34

JUNE 2008

*H*arold stood by the car, and Chloe got out and came around to join him as Danny walked over, appearing he was in utter turmoil. Harold was not sure if it would have been preferable to have him looking irate as opposed to what he saw now because this sure seemed as if it was going to be an emotional and uncomfortable scene he absolutely did not want to have to go through. He had never been so good at confrontations that involved emotional upset for as long as he could remember. Chloe was better at that kind of thing, but on the heels of what she had just gone through back in Hampton, he did not want to put the responsibility with dealing with Danny as he was now on her shoulders. Harold exhaled and braced himself, hoping to get through it as quickly as possible and without too much rancor and bitterness once they had explained their situation to him.

"Hi, guys," Danny began, looking as if he had not slept all night. "I just got your message. Can we talk?"

Harold nodded, figuring after how available and open Danny had been with them up to his point, that being upfront and honest with him was the let they could do. He felt bad enough as it was about not honoring his oral agreement with Jonathan. He did not want to add to it. They walked over to the small patio out front and sat around the iron, oval table off to one side.

"You were pretty vague on the phone, but I gather from your urgency that you must feel strongly about going back home."

Harold was unsure how much detail to go into, considering how skeptical they knew Danny was about anything paranormal. Maybe, he thought, he could just dance around what they had seen the night before without going into it all and having the man think them insane.

"We do," Harold replied. "Circumstances have arisen since we got here that we didn't anticipate when we took the jobs with Jonathan that have made us wary about continuing."

"Any problems with the kids or Tony or something or one of his guys?"

Chloe jumped in, seeing how hard this was becoming for Harold. "No, no, no, Danny, nothing like that. Adam and Katie are wonderful. And trust me, it's killing me to know I will be leaving them in a lurch once again, especially since we really seemed to be making progress getting them back on track."

Harold picked up the baton at that point. "And I'm

fine with Tony and his guys. The work has been interesting, and we all seemed to be meshing well."

Danny furrowed his brow, and a look of crushing defeat began to come over his expression. "Then I guess I don't understand. I mean, if it's the money or something, I can always talk with Jonathan and see if we can bump that up."

"It's not the money either, Danny."

"Then help me out here, guys. I certainly respect your position, but I'm at a loss as to what's going on. I know the kids love you, Chloe, and I've heard nothing but raves from Tony about all you have done, Harold, by stepping in and offering your expertise in the renovations."

Harold looked to Chloe, and she nodded slightly, letting him know they had been backed into a corner in this conversation regarding what had made them finally decide they might be in danger if they stayed any longer after having had the encounter with Teresa the night before. Harold sighed in resignation, now seeing they had no choice as well, and he forged ahead despite knowing Danny's opinions on anything paranormal or supernatural. Otherwise, they would just look impulsive, fickle, and professionally unreliable.

"Okay, Danny, here's what's going on," Harold replied. With some reluctance, Harold told Danny about how Adam and Katie had reported to Chloe having seen a vision of their mother.

"We didn't think anything of it initially," Chloe added. "I just figured it was some coping mechanism in helping them get over her death. Like these imaginary friends, they have created. It was a bit unsettling when they both said they had seen her, but then again, I know they have been through severe trauma."

"You worried the kids are maybe...I don't know... needing professional help and you don't feel able or qualified to offer it?" Danny asked, still looking perplexed.

"There's more," Harold replied.

In much detail and drawing from his memory of what had been a pretty shocking experience for them both from the night before, Harold let Danny know they had been confronted with what they were sure was Teresa Thompson's ghost as well. Danny looked at them, his mouth agape in an open *O*.

"You're kidding, right?" he finally said in as gentle and non-accusatory tone as possible.

Harold and Chloe shook their heads.

"We know how you feel on this subject, Danny, but we saw what we saw. Also, Chloe has had her own independent experience with things like this in the past, so we're not quite so skeptical about the possibility, I'm afraid. With that coming on the heels of the stories that are floating around in Green Pond, we're just concerned for our safety."

Danny nodded and paused as if he were considering how to respond. "Obviously, we're on different pages on the validity of the paranormal," Danny began. "But I do respect your opinion, even if I don't buy into any of that. It's not that I'm saying supernatural events don't happen. I just have never seen anything or had such an experience to make me a believer. For the sake of argument, let's assume that this type of thing is real and you did see Teresa. Are you thinking she's coming back to lead someone to her killer?"

Harold shrugged. "No idea, Danny. But right now, with these two issues, we're really uncomfortable here."

Danny nodded again. "Look, I have absolutely no idea who did kill Teresa. And I'm well familiar with the stuff that comes out of Green Pond, thinking that Jonathan had some hand in it. Knowing my brother as well as I do and what he is and is not capable of, I just find that accusation ludicrous. I would suggest that the stress and pressure you have been under, both from back in Hampton and now here, has perhaps made you see something that wasn't there. You heard this story from Adam and Katie, then you bumped into a local, Ralph Yardley, I'm guessing since he's the main proponent of this myth, and your minds have played tricks on your eyes."

"All I can say, Danny," Harold replied, "is that we saw what we saw. It sure didn't seem like a hallucination or anything at the time."

"I'm sure it didn't. But I also know this old place has a lot of weird and odd nooks and crannies that can make the light do things that can fool you. It's happened to me from time to time as well."

Harold did not reply, not wanting to argue the point that the wide flight of stairs was hardly a "nook or cranny." An uncomfortable silence fell over them all until Danny spoke up at last. He knew what he was about to say next was perhaps unfair and a little unscrupulous, but Jonathan needed them badly.

"I will honor whatever decision you make, guys," Danny said. "I would never want you to feel unsafe or vulnerable in any way here. But, if you leave now, it's going to create a situation that I'm not sure I know how to deal with." He paused to think and was obviously struggling with his feelings. "I'm sure I don't need to go into great detail and explain just how tenuous everything is here at the mansion just now. Following Teresa's murder, Jonathan nearly had to be committed. The kids were practically catatonic as well, and though they are back on the road now—mostly due to Chloe's efforts—it's like watching someone teetering on the top of a fence and trying to figure out which way they might fall if they lose their balance so you can catch them before they do.

"I came back sooner than I had planned when Tony let me know just how bad everything was. It seems as if my presence has been a bit of a stabilizing force for them all, but I'm afraid that you leaving might put everything back right where it was when I first arrived."

Harold flexed his jaw muscles as he was not keen on being made to feel responsible for what happened to this family. It was sad, but it was not like he was personally responsible.

"I know this is unfair, guys," Danny went on, "but we really need you now. Jonathan seems more and more likely to just sell off the place when all the work is done, just be rid of all the bad memories here. So the sooner we get there, the better. I know Tony is counting on Harold. It's not like we can find qualified help in Green Pond or elsewhere at the moment, and I feel like Adam and Katie just need another nudge to get them over the last hump they're facing to deal with their own trauma."

Chloe sighed and looked away, feeling like she was in the showroom facing a used car salesman who prided himself on the hard-sell technique and an inevitable close.

"I'm begging you, guys," Danny finally said. "Please just give it a few more days. If anything else happens like what has arisen to freak you out, just come to me, and we can go our separate ways. But for right now, please just reconsider. I can't hold this place together on my own."

Harold looked to Chloe as he watched Danny actually wipe away a tear from his face. It was not like he was an unemotional stone himself, and Danny's uninhibited show of emotion cut to his heart. She sighed again and nodded to Harold.

"Okay, Danny," Harold replied at last, "it's a deal. But if anything else like this comes our way, there will be no negotiation, all right? I won't put Chloe in a position of danger."

Danny smiled weakly and thanked them profusely before going back to his car and taking off. Harold and Chloe lugged their stuff back inside and upstairs to their room, wondering if they had just made a big mistake...

35

JULY 2008

A couple weeks went by following their conversation with Danny, and nothing even closely resembling the visit from Teresa had happened. Harold went back to work side by side with Tony, and Chloe continued her efforts with Adam and Katie. The kids made small steps each day as more and more of what Chloe had been told of their old personalities bubbled to the surface. They were still not all the way back, she thought. She still found them occasionally lapsing into periods of silence and sullenness that she had seen when she arrived, but now they were short in duration, and for the most part, they were talkative, happy, and outgoing. On some days, Chloe had the feeling the three of them had known each other for years rather than just months. They were great kids underneath the damage.

In their "classroom," they were making progress as well. Both Adam and Katie were naturally bright and motivated to learn, and Chloe saw that all they had needed was a little push. The fallout from Teresa's death and the revolving door of nannies had taken their toll. Her persistence and constancy, Chloe figured, had been just as helpful as anything specific she had done in the education department. Putting herself in their shoes, Chloe could see how hard it would be to have a normal routine—or even want to have one—with all those distractions and inconsistencies.

As well, the renovations were chugging along, and Tony told everyone he could finally see a definite light at the end of the tunnel for a finished product. Harold loved being a part of the renewed efforts, and even as skilled and talented as he was, he was learning new things from Tony, techniques he otherwise might never have been exposed to and could use in his own business when they went back to Hampton. And to top it all off, when Harold checked in back in Hampton, just to make sure there was nothing he needed to take care of personally, Madeline assured him all was well. Revenues were holding steady, and they were getting frequent calls from potential new clients based on recommendations from former ones.

With their lives back on a more normal keel, the only issue that still troubled Harold and Chloe was whether or not there was any real validity to whether Jonathan had had anything to do with Teresa's murder. The overall dynamic in Green Pond was odd. Danny swore up and down that even considering for a minute that Jonathan might be capable of such a thing was ridiculous, while the more people they talked to in town, they found the prevailing opinion to be just the opposite. Both Harold and Chloe knew this was really none of their business, but it was one of those things, kind of like an annoying hangnail, that you just wanted to be resolved one way or the other.

Late at night, they often discussed the bits and pieces they had:

Danny's assurance that Jonathan was innocent

Gossip from town that Jonathan was involved, even if he had not killed her himself

Despite Danny's disbelief in it, the visit from Teresa Thompson, leaving them with the feeling she wanted help in solving her murder

The overheard conversation from Jonathan's office possibly indicating he was planning on cashing out his investments and fleeing Green Pond

Lack of any real emotion from Jonathan over Teresa's death...or any real emotion at all other than his businesses

But in the end, they looked back on Danny's heartfelt plea to them to stay on and eventually forgot all about their curiosity over the real truth. After all, they were not cops or private detectives. Besides, even if they did move ahead with their idea of sitting down and talking directly with Jonathan to get his side of it all, he never seemed to be around. Since their last sitdown with Danny, he had been making extra efforts to make sure they had everything they needed and that nothing—no matter how slight or insignificant—had happened to make them want to reconsider.

Before giving up on the idea completely, though,

they discussed maybe getting Danny to set up a meeting with Jonathan for them, assuming he was more in the know on his brother's comings and goings. But two objections, one from Chloe and one from Harold, nixed the whole idea.

Danny might feel slighted that they would go around him to talk to Jonathan since he had made himself so available to them and had been so kind. Why would they want to speak to him instead?

And any inquiry might offend Jonathan himself and really put them in danger if he were guilty.

At the moment, things were running like a well-oiled machine, and it seemed that any intervention from them might do more harm than good, regardless of Jonathan's involvement. And quite frankly, other than a vague and still-unknown reason for Teresa's visit, all they had to suggest that Jonathan had anything to do with the murder was gossip from town and a conversation Chloe might very well have misinterpreted. Chloe agreed with Harold that the strategy, for now, should be "let sleeping dogs lie."

* * *

BUT ABOUT A WEEK LATER, Chloe was working with Adam and Katie on a math assignment she had given them when she heard some off sounds coming from down the hall. It reminded her of the time they had stumbled across Danny moving boxes around, but this time the noise seemed to be coming from Jonathan's private office—the one where she had overheard the conversation that had made her think he was cashing out to flee town. She told the kids to keep working while she stepped out for a minute to investigate. As she moved closer, it was not the sound of crates being relocated but the simple creak of the office door. She knew Tony had made every effort to look at every last detail of the renovation, but apparently, he had missed oiling the old hinges on that door.

Ordinarily, that would never have given her a second moment's consideration, but Jonathan always kept that door locked when he was away—from observation, she had seen him chastise workers when they had gone inside without permission. And she knew he had left two days ago for yet another meeting of business partners in Dallas. Never one to just let her curiosity ride, Chloe crept closer in case someone might have broken in while they were all busy with their day's chores. The door was ajar, but she heard nothing coming from inside the room. She figured intruders would be making more of a racket. *Maybe Jonathan came back unannounced once again? Or maybe this one time, he didn't latch it properly and an errant breeze has simply pushed open the door an inch or two.*

But as she moved closer, this latter possibility seemed impossible as the hallway was still, and the air outside was especially stagnant and sultry all morning. She had been praying for even a brief passing breeze to offer some relief to the stuffy room where she and the kids had been working. Though her brain told her to just turn around and go back to the kids, Chloe could not help herself. She would walk on by and glance in. If

Jonathan were there, she would just ignore him and act as if she had been going to the kitchen. But if he was not there, then she needed to close and latch the door, making sure no one had broken in. She set off, looking off furtively to her right as she passed the gap—no one was there.

She stepped back just to close and relatch the door as she had planned, but when she looked across the room, she saw an array of papers strewn across Jonathan's desk. The man was, in her experience anyway, genetically predisposed to absolute order and neatness. The messy condition of the desk seemed highly irregular, and Chloe decided to check it out just in case someone might have broken in and then left when they heard her coming down the hall. All the lights were off, leaving the only light coming into the dim room, the sun from the window just behind the desk itself. Chloe felt nervous and conspicuous as she walked over, but the situation just did not feel right. Without a break-in, there was no way—barring some sort of emergency—that Jonathan would have left this mess behind.

When she walked around behind the desk, it became even more baffling and bewildering. From odds and ends of the papers she could read, Chloe began to poke through some of the documents. There on the desk, for anyone to easily see and look through, was a vast array of all sorts of financial papers related to all of Jonathan's various investments. Chloe was no expert on such things, but what she could see were official-looking documents of outstanding loans, old and revised wills, a prospectus or two for some stocks, and many other things that she figured you had to be a seasoned accountant or financial advisor to understand. She immediately released the corner of the one paper she had in her hand, dropping it to the desk as if it might bite her.

Chloe found her heart pounding away as she quickly exited the room and headed for the kitchen for a glass of water. *What has she stumbled into?*

36

JULY 2008

*C*hloe stood, staring out through the large window over the kitchen sink as a red wing hawk hovered over the trees, riding the thermals in the afternoon heat. She set down the empty glass after having gulped its contents nervously, nearly having it slip through her shaky fingers and onto the floor. Everything she and Harold had tossed back and forth and bandied about concerning Jonathan when they had decided he was in the clear over having had anything to do with Teresa's murder had just been wiped away in one quick brush as far as she was concerned. She wondered if it might have been better had she had not let her curiosity guide her just then and been in the dark as to what was there. But knowing or not, what she had seen sure indicated something was seriously amiss here…and Chloe certainly did not adhere to the old adage of "ignorance is bliss."

To begin with, if all were well, there was no way Jonathan would have just left all of what she deemed very sensitive, personal financial information out in the open for anyone to have access to, even if the room had been locked up as was the norm. All of his account numbers and details of each investment were wide open, allowing anyone to have come along and just stolen anything they might have wanted. *Is it possible someone just photographed or otherwise copied what they needed before she got there?* Regardless, she shuddered at what was even worse than the security risk Jonathan had put himself at over his finances. What she had seen seemed to back up the phone conversation she had overheard a few weeks prior.

Even with her limited understanding of it, Chloe saw that Jonathan indeed was moving large amounts between accounts, consolidating the majority of his holdings into a few. She still had no real proof of his strategy but added to what she had overheard in her eavesdropping session, it seemed there was no other conclusion to be drawn but that he had plans to make just a few large withdrawals of cash before fleeing. To her, that meant he had to be guilty on some level. Either he had become aware that someone had uncovered new information that would point a finger at him, or he was being proactive and just running before that might happen. Chloe knew it was an enormous leap in logic, but no other possibility seemed likely to her at the moment.

Maybe having her here to take care of Adam and Katie and Harold to work on the mansion's renovations had all been just a cover for him. Chloe looked at all the disparate dots now, and she drew up in her mind what she believed to have happened. Before she lost her nerve, Chloe went looking for Harold to fill him in on her discovery in Jonathan's office and how she now saw what his big picture plan might have been all along. But one of Tony's guys told her that Harold had driven into town with their boss for a load of lumber. Chloe gathered her wits and decided that really thinking it over before unloading it on anyone, even Harold, might be a wise move.

Perhaps seeing her theory in writing might give her a better and not so overly emotional view of what she suspected. Chloe set the kids up with an activity in their room and then went to the small desk in the old library and wrote out what she saw as a logical and reasoned interpretation of what Jonathan had planned.

1. Something yet to be uncovered had transpired between Jonathan and Teresa, and it was serious enough for him to know she had to be done away with.

2. Jonathan created this public story of an out-of-town trip as an alibi to cover himself during the time Teresa was killed. This had been so well-crafted that even Danny declared it to be solid. Whether or not he had done it himself or hired it out, she did not know. She did not know Jonathan well enough to know if he was cold-blooded enough to commit murder or not, but certainly, he had adequate financial means to hire someone if necessary.

3. Now that Teresa was out of the way, Jonathan had gone to great lengths to make those close to him see him as having nearly been incapacitated by her death. He wanted the partially finished mansion to be wrapped up so he could theoretically sell it off and remove himself from a deep, emotional scar in his life—a very believable ploy, Chloe thought—and one both they and Danny seemed to have bought into. That was where she and Harold came in. No one anywhere in Green Pond would deny that Adam and Katie meant the world to Jonathan. So having her there to take care of them fit into that part of his scheme, as did Harold's role as Tony's partner to complete the mansion and prepare it for sale.

She sat back and drank deeply from her wine to dampen her parched throat and calm her nerves after getting her thoughts all down in black and white. She read it over a few times just to make sure she had not omitted any detail that might add to her line of suspicion and further support her interpretation. She made a few minor changes in the wording and added one or two touches that she recalled as she reviewed the page, but overall it looked perfect.

After her final read-through, Chloe had no doubts that Jonathan was responsible. She did not know his specific plan for abandoning Green Pond and how Adam and Katie might fit into his overall strategy. She could not imagine he would put them in any danger if what everyone in town said about how Jonathan put the kids above all else were true. Then again, if he felt cornered or felt he had no escape from the authorities once they became aware of his actions, it was hard to say how he would react or what he might resort to. Even as awful as it sounded, Chloe supposed he might just leave them behind if he felt he had no other option.

The day wore on, and Harold still had not returned as Chloe paced and fretted and could not calm down.

She really wanted to get Harold's opinion and feed-back, but if what she suspected ended up being true, then time was of the essence. Too much of a delay in taking any action might be dangerous as well, not just for them but for Adam and Katie as well. Though it was not her first choice and highly impulsive and rash as well, Chloe decided to go looking for Jonathan on her own and confront him just as they had originally discussed. She was afraid that by the time Harold returned and had a chance to review what she had written out and then they talked it over, that Jonathan might well be on his way to freedom.

37

JULY 2008

*B*ut a thorough search of the grounds proved fruitless. Jonathan, as was usually the case lately, was nowhere to be found. Whether or not that meant he was out of town again or just making himself scarce as the potential date of his escape from Green Pond approached, Chloe did not know. Even in her frustration at not finding him, she realized just how foolish that plan had been and was actually thankful he had not been around. Chloe knew herself well enough to know just how impulsive she could be at times. She took an objective look at the situation and realized she had become overly obsessed with proving Jonathan guilty. In her zeal for pursuing this, she had pushed aside just how dangerous and risky that move could have been had she actually found him and had the confrontation.

She had let her emotions get the better of her and completely blocked out the ramifications of what might have occurred to any of them if Jonathan were indeed guilty. If he *were* a murderer or even an accomplice, what would be the big deal in a few more? Chloe went to the solarium and spent a few minutes doing some of the deep breathing techniques Dr. Abrams had taught her when she felt overly stressed or like she was coming unglued.

This was not quite that situation, but as she sat and pulled deep breaths in and out of her lungs, her eyes closed, imagining a peaceful spot on a tropical island—the visualization she and Dr. Abrams had come up with together to help her get centered when need be—Chloe felt like based on circumstances that she had just dodged a bullet. She was not an especially religious person, but at that moment, Chloe felt as if a guardian angel had been looking out for her. It would have served no one had she prematurely jumped the gun and caused Jonathan to turn on them if he felt threatened. When she was done, Chloe had not changed her mind about eventually speaking with Jonathan. There was no way to avoid that if they were to get to the bottom of the mystery but minimizing any potential dangers had to be part of that plan. And that meant talking to Harold. It was not fair to move ahead on this without his inclusion, and he might actually see a part of her missive that changed everything.

In order to clear her mind and put some distance between this sense of urgency, Chloe thought maybe another hike in the woods with Adam and Katie might be good. The kids loved them, and she knew the exercise and fresh air would likely be just as beneficial for her as well. After putting her notes in a safe place, she left the library and headed up the corridor to find the kids and see if they might be up for a short hike before the sun set. They were very good at just being self-entertained, and she assumed they were in their room, playing yet another game they seemed to have no end at creating.

But before she took more than a couple of steps in that direction, Chloe was distracted by what sounded like someone rummaging around in the cellar. It was unlikely that Adam and Katie were down there playing, as she was sure she would have seen them walk by here earlier. Then again, she had been quite focused on writing up a summary for Harold, and maybe they had slipped by her during her search for Jonathan. She reversed her direction and headed for the kitchen to access the door that led to the cellar to check it out. A dingy, dank, cold, concrete cellar seemed an odd place for them to want to play, but that was likely just colored by her own experiences as a young girl. As Chloe's hand touched the cellar doorknob and she eased it open, she flicked on the switch just to the left at the top of the stairs, which gave the flight enough illumination for her to make her way down. As the light came on, she was instantly transported back to being about eight years old and in her childhood home again.

Even as a kid, Chloe had been filled with this seemingly insatiable ability to control her curiosity. "Chloe the Cat," her father had called her as a joke. And one afternoon, when she was just bouncing around the house, looking for anything to entertain her or amuse her until it was time for her afternoon snack, Chloe wandered down into the old basement of their Amherst, Virginia, house. The dark recesses and sour odors of the poorly ventilated cellar had never bothered her, and Chloe had often used trips down there to create adventures and games of her own like she was some explorer wandering the undiscovered chambers of some long-forgotten civilization.

And that day was no different. Chloe walked around the room using the narrow path between the furnace and some shelves that her father had built to store things. She came around the other side and moved forward, approaching a small room with a separate enclosure from the main base-ment. It had been, at one time, her parents had said, an old root cellar used by the original owners. Now it was just an empty space. Maybe eight feet square that just held a few moldy cardboard cartons that seemed unimportant. But to Chloe, sliding the door open against the grainy debris of the floor was a secret chamber she had found on this "expedi-tion" she was playing at.

She pulled on the string cord that hung down from a naked overhead bulb, and the weak light filled the room with a dim but adequate shine to let her see. Chloe walked farther inside and pretended she saw mounds of treasures and untold other artifacts. In her game, she was the first person to find this place since it had been abandoned eons ago. After having satisfied herself that she had gotten everything out of the experience that she could and was ready to call it quits and head back upstairs to see what her mother had waiting for her to eat, Chloe spotted an odd recess where two walls came together.

It looked like the old concrete had just degraded over

time, leaving a crumbling gap. But she went over anyway and poked the hole with an old stick she had picked up along the way. Before she knew it, an enormous mass of small, black spiders came racing out and scampered across the stick and then over her arm and were soon all over her. Chloe dropped the stick, screaming at the top of her lungs as she frantically tried to brush them away. But the more she swatted at the spiders, the more they seemed to cling to her, and more seemed to somehow make their way onto her skin.

In a total panic and flailing her arms as wildly as she could, Chloe came stumbling and tripping out of the room before falling to her knees as she screamed, feeling as if she were about to die. The spiders were on her arms, her legs, and even in her hair, making their way under her clothes before her father arrived, having heard her cries for help. He scooped her up and stripped her of her clothes as he rushed her to the large sink in the basement, where he often cleaned tools and paintbrushes from various household tasks. He got the water on and used the spray nozzle to wash away the spiders that were still remaining after his own attempts to free her of them. Even as he was working, Chloe continued to cry and scream, imagining they were still crawling all over her.

She had eventually calmed down as her father held her tight and reassured her that she was fine. But later on, even years after that day, Chloe refused to go in the cellar ever again unless her mother or father went along. Her fear of spiders stayed with her well into her teenage years before she overcame that phobia. But her dislike and avoidance of spiders had never gone away completely.

As irrational as she knew it was, she always

summoned Harold to kill any spider she came across at home. They just gave her the creeps. And that was what flooded her imagination now as she stood at the top of the steps and looked into the dim recesses below as her heart raced. *Why, oh why did the kids have to go down there to play?*

38

JULY 2008

*C*hloe took a deep breath, pushed aside that old memory as best she could, and stepped down onto the first stair, grimacing as it groaned audibly under her weight. She moved slowly, but with each successive step, she felt more at ease, and soon that old film in her head of that day faded to nothing. But oddly, as she got about halfway down, Chloe noticed that whatever it was she had heard earlier was now gone. All that remained, other than her heartbeat, was the creak of the wood under her feet. She called out to Adam and Katie as she neared the bottom of the flight, but no one answered. And as she stood on the cellar floor, there was no sign of them anywhere, nor was there any indication they might have been there playing.

In fact, once Chloe took the whole scene in, it looked to her as if nothing here had been touched in years. Apparently, the cellar was at the bottom of Tony's renovation priority list. Just to make sure there was not something else amiss, Chloe swallowed her childhood fears and moved on. She wove her way around an obstacle course of wooden crates and cardboard boxes, some of which were still taped up as if they had not been opened since they had been shipped, while others just had the top flaps overlapped as if they had been opened and then just closed up for convenience. Old tools hung from various spots on the rafters, looking as if they had not been used in some time, either. A serious coat of dust, grime, and even mildew was covering just about everything. It was not as bad as spiders, Chloe thought, but it was gross all the same.

As she made her way around the contents, the light from the overhead bulb began to lose its effectiveness, and Chloe pulled out the small penlight she had begun to carry with her everywhere. With all the construction going on, she had learned the hard way not to go without it in case Tony had to shut off the power with no warning for some wiring work. Chloe switched it on and panned the beam ahead as she ducked, avoiding a huge tangle of cobwebs that hung low from some of the weight-bearing supports of the house. She straightened and looked off to her right before she froze in place, gasping briefly. On the wall there, she found an old door that had seen better days. A rusty and broken padlock hung from the hinge that looked as if it could fall out of its setting at any time.

Chloe thought immediately of that small room in the basement of her childhood home but was able to brush it off as just a coincidence. In retrospect, Chloe could not say why she felt the need to see what was on the other side of the door based on what was buried in her memory banks from childhood, but sometimes it seemed her curiosity was just impossible to silence. She was expecting the door to be quite resistant to movement based on the overall condition of the cellar and the rusty hinge and lock, but once she tossed the lock aside, she found it to swing open easily as if it had been well-used all this time.

Chloe stood in the opening and moved the beam of light around to discover what looked like a hidden or maybe secret room, not quite as large as the average bedroom in a house. It was eerily reminiscent of the one where she had grown up, but she held her ground. She stepped inside slowly and panned her light over the left wall, where she found a small cabinet that looked surprisingly well-preserved relative to everything else down there. It was made of wood but seemed to have held up a bit better over time. Maybe being closed off in this dark space had helped; she had no idea. The top drawer was slightly open, and Chloe went over, and with some effort, slid it open and looked inside.

The drawer itself was empty other than what looked like an old leather-bound book, which she removed from the drawer. The leather was cracked and split in places and had fallen victim to an attack of mildew like she had encountered earlier. She pulled the long sleeve of her shirt over her hand and used it to wipe away the gunk on the cover. There in large, gold-embossed print on the lower right-hand corner of the cover was:

Teresa Thompson

2000-

Chloe felt her pulse race as she just stared at the writing, wondering if she was seeing things. Had she actually stumbled across some sort of diary Teresa had been keeping and then hiding away to keep it secret?

* * *

WITH THE DISCOVERY of what Chloe was sure was the secret diary of Teresa Thompson, she canceled any thoughts she had previously entertained of a hike with the kids. Seeing what was inside that book was too important. She let Adam and Katie know they were free for the rest of the afternoon and that she would see them at dinner.

"Just stay inside, or if you want to go out, don't wander off. Stay close by; it will be dark soon, okay?"

Adam and Katie nodded and ran off, squealing with delight at having been offered free time. Wanting as much privacy a possible, Chloe retreated to the solarium, where she doubted any workers would be. She carefully opened the fragile cover, and before she knew it, she was completely immersed in the detailed narrative of Teresa's life at Aberdeen Estates. Her entries were a very personal and intimate record of all her feelings and thoughts of all that was going on around her. Chloe guessed that with Jonathan away so much—if that were to be believed anyway—Teresa needed some outlet to express herself. It was heart-wrenching to read about a woman who was feeling increasingly isolated and lonely while having to wear the façade of being strong and holding it all together for an absent spouse.

But the further into the diary that Chloe got, the really disturbing sense she got was that Teresa might be growing progressively more paranoid by the week. Her writing, at one point, seemed to devolve into nothing more than a disparate and random collection of ramblings, almost just a stream of consciousness kind of thing. With that tone added, it was hard to know if what she was writing had any real validity or not. Just prior to her murder and making up most of the final entries in her diary was the repeated and emphasized feeling from Teresa that something awful and nefarious was heading her way. She was short on the specifics as well as who she felt might be responsible for making her feel that way.

Chloe did not have any experience with such mental health possibilities, but from her own depression and feelings of having no reason to keep on living after losing her baby, she knew well that anyone could fall into a deep, black hole if they let that inner voice that uttered such ideas speak loudly enough. From work with Dr. Abrams, Chloe had come to understand that an inner voice can be helpful as well as harmful. You had to really discern the message and know that making you feel worthless or unwanted was not your true intuition or true inner guide. That was, Dr. Abrams had told Chloe, a version of what the innovative psychologist, M. Scott Peck had described in his landmark book, *The People of the Lie,* back in the 1980s.

It was not quite a direct analogy, but Chloe got her point after reading the book. Your intuition or inner guide—whatever you wanted to call it—was always there to help and protect you, never to demean you and drag you down. Once she had combined that understanding with the individualized sessions, Chloe had begun to improve dramatically. She wondered if what Teresa had penned here was like that, or maybe despite her ramblings toward the end, what she sensed was all very real?

Even without any details or specific names, the whole experience of reading Teresa's diary now, knowing what had actually befallen her, made Chloe shiver. Had Teresa just *sensed* that her life was in real danger, or had she actually found out that was the case but did not know how or who to reach out to? In any case, that solidified the situation for Chloe. Though Teresa had not spelled out exactly who she feared, there was no doubt in Chloe's mind that it had to be Jonathan. There was just too much incriminating evidence piling up for her to consider any other option. Now more than ever, Chloe was thankful she had not found Jonathan on-site in Harold's absence. With him obviously capable and very likely—at least in her mind—of killing Teresa, Chloe knew she would not have been long for the world had she confronted him on her own.

When she looked up, Chloe realized she had let time get away from her. It was turning dark, and she could hear Harold calling for her to come to dinner. She really must have made herself quite hidden in the jungle of the solarium, Chloe thought to herself as it seemed Harold had no idea where she was. Chloe closed the diary and tucked it away in their room before answering him and heading downstairs to join everyone. This was all very explosive evidence in her eyes, and she knew Harold would see it that way as well. But for now, she had to keep it to herself. She could not appear as if anything was going on with her or that anything had changed despite everything she had unearthed that day. Chloe hoped she could pull that off. Any unintended signal might be deadly for them all.

39

JULY 2008

*C*hloe stopped off at a mirror in the hallway just before heading down to the dining room and took a few quick seconds to try to make sure she was not looking as excited and eager as she was inside about her day. Acting had never been her strong suit, and more than once, friends had pointed out that it was a good thing she was not a gambler, as she had a really lousy poker face. She exhaled and went down, determined to do the best she could. She knew she had to contain herself until she could get Harold alone to fill him in. Fortunately, Tony looked completely wiped out from his day and appeared to be struggling just to stay awake long enough to eat. He had zero interest in how Chloe looked.

As well, the kids were bubbling and chatty, going on and on about these cool little rocks they had found while playing outside that afternoon, and everyone seemed to be letting them steer the conversation. Chloe was relieved, as all she had to do was get through dinner and then get the kids to bed. Also, it was wonderful to see Adam and Katie so excited and engaged in just that simple discovery of their own. To Chloe, it meant they were well on their way back to normal, though with what she now suspected about their father, she could not help but be concerned as to what might become of them when the truth came out.

In her mind, the worst-case scenario is that Jonathan might flee with them in tow, which might destroy them completely. Or...if somehow he just fleas, leaving them behind, will Danny be willing and able to take them in and care for them properly? Though keeping herself and Harold safe was still her priority, Chloe could not help worrying about Adam and Katie as well. She had just gotten so attached to them in the few months she had been taking care of them. As all these thoughts filled her mind, Chloe kept glancing at her watch. Dinner seemed to be taking hours. Finally, Adam and Katie were excused from the table and ran off to get ready for bed as Chloe promised to be up in just a few minutes to tuck them in and get a closer look at the collection of rocks they had talked about all evening.

She felt as if she could hardly sit still as Reggie cleared the dishes, and she and Harold were left with just coffee. Overall, she thought she had stayed as calm and in control as possible considering the circumstances, but when Reggie disappeared into the kitchen with the last load of dishes from dinner, Harold looked at Chloe with a confused expression before he set down his coffee cup.

"Okay, Chloe," he began calmly, "what the hell is going on with you tonight?"

Chloe blanched, caught off-guard by his observation, but then not so shocked when she realized how well he knew her. Still, she was not comfortable saying too much until they were alone.

"What do you mean?"

"Come on, Chloe, I know you. If anyone is a worse actor than me, it's you. You've been like a cat on a hot tin roof all through dinner, looking at your watch like every five minutes, glancing around suspiciously. Let's hear it."

Chloe blushed, embarrassed he had so easily seen through her ruse when she had been positive she had been so clever. A tinge of anxiety rippled through her as she wondered if anyone else had picked up on it but had just been too polite to inquire.

"Not here, Harold. I had a big day. I mean a *big* day, with a capital *B*. But I don't want to go into it until we are alone in our room, okay?" she whispered in case Reggie was coming back to make sure he had gathered everything up.

"Okay, but you're being very mysterious, I must say. Did I do something to upset you?"

"Oh, hell no, Harold, nothing like that. Just hang on until I can get the kids to bed."

He nodded, but now the cryptic explanation had him more on edge and curious than before. Chloe was one of those people who was always even-keeled—her recent depression excepted—but whatever was going on with her, it was *way* out of character.

* * *

HAROLD WENT into the kitchen to keep Reggie company while he finished up, agreeing to meet Chloe in about an hour or so back in their room, giving her time to get the kids calmed down from their own exciting day and tucked in for the night. Like everyone else at the mansion Harold was interacting with, he found Reggie delightful and loved it when they both had some free time to just hang out and chat. In addition to being what Harold considered a world-class chef—though Reggie vehemently denied that compliment when Harold had said so earlier—he found the slightly mysterious man to possess a wealth of knowledge on various topics.

Harold had heard of the expression "Renaissance Man," and as far as he was concerned, that title fit Reggie to a tee, even though he had never actually met one and was just guessing from his own impressions. Talking to him tonight was no exception, either, but with what Chloe had just laid on him as she took off to see to the kids, Harold was having trouble keeping his mind and his focus on their conversation. He was just too distracted and anxious to hear what she might have in store for him later. He finally excused himself, saying he was tired from the day, as he did not want Reggie to get the impression he was not listening to him and not interested in what he had to say.

In the meantime, Chloe was with Adam and Katie, trying to make a genuine effort to listen and make positive, encouraging chit-chat about this new collection of theirs. In and of itself, the collection was quite varied and impressive, and had Chloe's mind not been overly consumed with what her day had revealed, it would not have felt like such a chore to engage with them. On the one hand, she was thrilled that for the first time, Adam and Katie seemed so energized and excited about something of their own. She knew how vital it was to encourage and support that to keep them moving forward. But on the other hand, all she could think of was getting back to their room so she could tell Harold everything. It was like having two parts of her brain fighting for control of her. After a bit, she finally got them to put everything away, promising to go with them tomorrow so they could show her where they had found those cool rocks. By the time she tucked them in, said goodnight, and got back to their own room, she found Harold sitting on the bed. He had his shoes off and was leaning up against the headboard, sipping a beer. He handed her one as she moved across the room and joined him.

"I figured you could use one of these based on whatever it is you have waiting for me," Harold said.

"Thanks. Yeah, I could use it. I'm not sure where to even begin."

"I'm just glad your head didn't explode during dinner from trying to keep all of whatever this is inside. Take a deep breath and just start at the beginning, I guess."

Chloe laughed and nodded with him, took a long draw on the cold beer, and exhaled to shrug off her nervousness. There was so much to tell him, but she did not want to rush through any of it and maybe make it feel to him any less serious and believable than it was to her. And it was not like she just wanted Harold to rubber-stamp her interpretation of it all. Chloe wanted Harold's honest and objective opinion. If he was jumping to a dangerous conclusion based on her intuition and emotions, she wanted Harold to stop her before she leaped to the point of no return.

During dinner and after when she had been putting Adam and Katie to bed, Chloe had continued to analyze her day's findings from as many angles as she could think of. There was not one approach that she had taken that made her think for even a second that she was off base. But sometimes, you just needed a fresh set of eyes and ears to take a look as a final evaluation.

"Okay, Harold...from the beginning.... It all began early this morning when the kids were working on some mathematical brain-teasers I gave them to test how much they have picked up from my lessons in the last few days."

He sat back and let her tell her story. From the beginning, he could tell it was going to be worth the wait.

40

JULY 2008

*W*ith the slow, detailed, and deliberate way she had of explaining any situation, Chloe took Harold through her day. She led off with being drawn to a disturbance in Jonathan's office and how surprised she had been to find it not only unlocked and open but then coming across the disarray of sensitive financial documents on his desk. It did not appear to her as a break-in, though, just highly out of character for Jonathan knowing how guarded he was about that room. After getting over the initial surprise, she had then linked what she had come away with after a brief scan of a few of the papers she could understand with the phone conversation she had inadvertently eavesdropped on earlier.

"Both events seemed related."

"So you're convinced he's preparing to run to avoid a possible arrest?" Harold asked.

"Hang on. There's much more. Let me lay it all out, and then I want your take, okay?"

Harold nodded and indicated for her to go on. Chloe described how she had planned on taking the kids hiking again since they had been cooped up all day but got distracted by some noise coming from the cellar. She told how she had gone down there, thinking Adam and Katie might be messing around with the stuff down there, but when she went down, the noise ceased suddenly, and the kids were nowhere to be seen.

"Rats, maybe?" Harold suggested.

"Maybe, but it didn't sound like that to me. More just like someone rummaging around looking for something."

He nodded again, and Chloe went on to describe finding the small hidden room that had nothing inside but a single cabinet that held only an old, leather-bound book.

"Wow," Harold commented. "This is getting better by the minute."

"Just wait," Chloe replied with a grin.

He sat mesmerized as she told of finding what she eventually determined to be a diary belonging to Teresa Thompson that she had been keeping for several years. Chloe gave him a summary of what she felt was relevant to their situation now based on her most recent entries, including what she had concluded that it all meant to her—the phone call, the shifting of funds into just a few accounts for easy withdrawal, and the vague, often rambling, if not prescient observations of a possibly paranoid Teresa Thompson.

She handed him the outline of bullet points she had

come up with before going to the dresser where she had stashed the actual diary and handing it to him.

"That's my executive summary and the diary in full if you want to read it for yourself. I think I did a pretty good job of picking out the salient bits and making a convincing argument for suspecting Jonathan of her murder. Just one thing, Harold…."

He looked up as he took the paper and book from her.

"The last…oh…say six months or so of entries in the diary? The ones leading up to her murder? It's pretty depressing stuff, and in the end, it makes you feel as if she might have really gone off the rails."

"Her paranoia?"

Chloe nodded sadly.

"Perhaps that's how it reads," Harold replied, "but considering she got murdered, I'm not sure she was so paranoid after all."

Chloe raised her eyebrows and nodded. "I guess that's true. Anyway, that was my day. You and Tony were over in Green Pond when I put all this together, so I couldn't talk to you until now."

"Anyone else know?"

Chloe looked at him sheepishly. "Almost, but no. Just you and me for now."

"Almost?"

She reluctantly admitted that she had felt such a sense of urgency about it all that she had gone looking for Jonathan to talk to him directly.

"Chloe!" Harold exclaimed, "Do you have any idea how dangerous that was?"

She nodded and hung her head. "Yeah, I know it was stupid. I was just worried that if we waited too long, he might jump ship before we can find out if any of this means what I think it does. Fortunately, he was nowhere to be found, and after the fact, I realized how foolish that ploy was. I knew I needed you in on this first, regardless of how much time it took. I've beat myself up enough over my poor judgment already. Sorry."

"It's okay...nothing lost. It just scares me to think what might have happened if he *had* been here, is all."

"Me, too, Harold...not my finest hour."

"Okay...how about you give me a few minutes to look all of this over, and I can give you my take on it all. I don't discount your opinion or interpretation. I mean, you were the one to experience all of this first-hand after all, but it won't hurt to have me look at it all with my own perspective before we do anything more. Fair?"

Chloe nodded and downed the last of her beer before heading off to get ready for bed. When she came back, he was still reading intently, and she could see the look of empathy and concern on his face as he flipped page after page of the diary. She knew Harold well and had an idea that he was trying to wrap his head around the often difficult-to-follow narrative of the either disturbed or just plain terrified Teresa Thompson.

Chloe eased into bed and picked up her tablet to read a book she had been trying to finish for weeks now. She had an idea that it might end up being quite late before Harold had pored through the diary and her notes to make his own evaluation, but this was way too important to just wait on. Besides, until they came to some decisions, Chloe was sure sleep was just going to be out of reach for her.

41

JULY 2008

*C*hloe tried valiantly to read her book, but she just could not concentrate on it knowing Harold was reviewing everything she had uncovered. She was anxious for his feedback and opinion on her conclusions and soon found she was just reading the same few paragraphs over and over and still had no idea what it was she had read. Just as she had felt earlier at dinner when it seemed that time had slowed to a crawl, Chloe was getting antsy and suddenly impatient at how long it seemed to be taking him to review it. However, once she forced herself to relax and calm down, Chloe knew it was just a skewed perception on her part.

Finally, after what felt to her like hours—though in actuality it had only been about thirty minutes—Harold closed the diary and set both the book and her notes on the side table on his side of the bed. She did her best to wait on him to speak, but the anticipation was killing her. At last, she could no longer take the suspense.

"Well?" she asked. "What do you think?"

Harold took a breath and looked over at her. All of a sudden, Chloe did not have a good feeling about what he was about to say as she had come to know his facial expressions well over the years.

"First of all," Harold began, "this diary is an absolutely incredible discovery. It seems Teresa Thompson was indeed troubled and worried about what she felt was going on around her here in the days and maybe even weeks leading up to her eventual murder."

"But?" Chloe prodded.

"But I'm not sure the contents of the diary itself are convincing me to agree completely with your conclusions surrounding Jonathan and his part in her death."

Chloe sat stunned and silent for a beat. She had not expected him to just be jumping up and down and saying, *"Yes, we need to move on this right away!"* Who was she kidding? That was a lie she was telling herself just now, she knew. Chloe was sure that on top of the two incidents in Jonathan's office, the diary contents would seal it.

"You're kidding, right? I mean, am I missing something, or doesn't what she was secretly keeping a log of make everything I have come across in Jonathan's office a pretty open and shut case for his guilt?"

"It might, Chloe, but it's the tone and the way she wrote in the diary that gives me pause."

"I'm not following your logic here, Harold. Is it

because she doesn't specifically name Jonathan as who she was afraid of?"

"That would certainly help for sure. But to me, it is more that her state of mind seems in question. I know there's no way to find this out without really ruffling feathers here—and quite frankly, it's none of our business—but I wonder if maybe Teresa might have been on some sort of medication for the anxiety and stress she lays out in those pages."

"Like antidepressants or something?" Chloe replied.

That was exactly what Harold had been thinking but had been hesitant to come out and say it based on what Chloe had just been through back home after losing the baby. He did not want to venture back into that part of her own treatment in those days, which had, for a brief time, included just that as part of her recovery.

"Just a thought," Harold replied. "I mean, you have to admit that her writing toward the end there was quite hard to follow and at times seemed to just wander off into a world that had little, if anything, to do with her situation at the mansion."

Chloe nodded, knowing he had a good point. That had bothered her as well when she had first read the entries. "Even so, maybe she had good reason to write in such a desperate-sounding and helpless way, making her appear paranoid, with or without any meds. Her concerns did come true after all."

Harold nodded. "But that doesn't mean it was Jonathan. Without some other hard evidence, I'm afraid it's a pretty big jump to link her ramblings to what you have overheard and found in that office."

Chloe realized it was a take on the situation she had overlooked. She had become so obsessed with the idea of Jonathan's guilt and viewed everything with such a selective set of blinders that she wondered now if maybe Harold might have been instrumental in keeping her from having made a huge error.

"If only she had just given us a name," Chloe said out loud more to herself than to Harold.

"That certainly would have helped. But for now, I think we need to tread a bit more softly until there's something more concrete indicating Jonathan killed her."

Chloe reluctantly nodded, knowing he was thinking more logically than she was rather than letting his emotions take over, which she now saw she had been guilty of. But still, she was nagged by the prospect that if she *were* right, then Jonathan might skip town and get away with murder, not to mention what would become of Adam and Katie.

"I'm not completely ruling out the possibility that you're correct, Chloe, but right now, without something more, I'm leaning toward buying the version of Jonathan that Danny has given us. He does know the man better than anyone. I'm trying not to let the gossip from Green Pond make too much of an impact in comparison, I guess. And maybe all of Jonathan's financial moves of late have nothing to do with the murder. Maybe he does just want to take the kids and move away from all the bad memories like Danny said."

"Okay. Yeah, I see your side of this now. So now what?" Chloe asked.

"Well, I hate to say this with all the fallout that I know will inevitably come crashing down, but I'm not sure for our own safety and well-being that we should hang around here just waiting for the other shoe to drop and this impacts us."

"But I thought you were buying into Danny's view of his brother? That the talk from town was just that?"

"Overall, it makes more sense to me, but with everything else you have come across with the man and taking into account that visit from Teresa a few weeks back, I'm not sure I want to take any chances in case you *are* right."

Chloe said nothing.

"You're worried about Adam and Katie, huh?" Harold asked.

"Very."

"I get that, Chloe. I really do. I know how close you've become to them, but it does them no good if Jonathan is guilty, then finds out we know, and who knows what will happen then. I think, for now, we have to put ourselves first, regardless of how cold and cruel that may look. Maybe pass along all we have to some authority in Green Pond and let them take up the baton. If he is guilty, then this is a job for professionals, not us."

JULY 2008

*E*ven basically agreeing with Harold's assessment of the situation, Chloe could not drop her suspicions about Jonathan, sure that she was right, even without what she knew was the solid, tangible evidence that would nail him for good. She had been raised with a very strong sense of right and wrong, and she was having trouble accepting that he might not actually get the punishment he deserved. The phone call and the scattered financial papers, as well as the diary contents, were a strong pull for Chloe, but what was really making her sure she was correct was that encounter she and Harold had had with Teresa on the staircase that night.

Chloe was sure that Teresa's last look to them before she had vanished for good was much more than just to make her presence known. Woman to woman, Chloe felt that was a plea for help, that Teresa knew who was responsible and wanted them brought to justice. But she needed some assistance from the physical world that she somehow could not take care of herself. Chloe did not know why she felt that way, but it was too strong to just ignore. Chloe knew Teresa was the only witness to her murder, and she wanted to work with her to find out if it had been Jonathan or someone he might have hired.

But after their last discussion, Chloe knew she could not share that with Harold. What she needed was some reasonable excuse to get him to delay their departure from Aberdeen Estates until she could figure out how to make all her intuition and desire to find the killer all come together. After his perfectly framed rebuttal of her interpretation of the situation, Chloe knew it would sound crazy for her to try to get him to put off their leaving. If she were right, and Jonathan was responsible, they were in grave danger right now if any of what she had come across leaked back to him.

Chloe racked her brain to come up with some plan that she thought Harold might find acceptable. It seemed impossible until she thought of Danny. It was a long shot, she knew, but it was the only one she could think of that she thought Harold might acquiesce to. Much like putting together a lesson plan for the kids, Chloe mapped out a series of points to cover when she went to Harold to make her pitch. He was initially reluctant to even consider anything that would have them in the mansion any longer than was absolutely necessary, but he did listen to her with an open mind.

What Chloe pitched was to go and talk to Danny rather than Jonathan as the last effort to try to solve the mystery before just leaving. She emphasized how he had gone above and beyond to offer his help and assistance regardless of the issue. From what she had seen, Danny was likely to consider altering his opinion of his brother if they laid out all they had uncovered, even with his firm disbelief in the paranormal. Chloe saw this one last effort as a compromise that could protect them from being put in Jonathan's sights.

"You really can't let this go, can you?" Harold said.

"I guess not. Blame my parents for instilling such a strong sense of morality."

"Even talking to Danny is a risky move, Chloe."

She nodded. "I know. It's kind of a gamble between him taking a look at what we have and joining us or refusing to accept to believe any of it based on his strong love and devotion to Jonathan."

"Family can often be much stronger than what is right and wrong, Chloe."

"And I'm hoping based on our experience of Danny so far—how nice and accommodating he has been with us—that he would not try to ignore it just to protect Jonathan. I get a real sense of honor and high character with him."

"Me, too, but does the chance that your idea of approaching him and having him join us outweigh the downside? I guess that's the question."

"I would say so. Even if he doesn't buy our story, I figure he will just say we're seeing something not there. And maybe he has some knowledge of the financial stuff I stumbled into that will explain it all—other reasons that Jonathan would be shifting funds around that we know nothing about."

Harold did not reply right away, but Chloe could see he was seriously considering her proposal. Harold held just as strong a sense of justice as she did. It was one of the things that had drawn her to him long ago. He was a man of his word and always did what he could to right wrongs he came across. After a brief silence, Harold reluctantly agreed to go along with her plan.

"Okay, Chloe, we'll give this a shot. I'm not 100% convinced it'll work, but if there's any chance it will, then we should try. Just one condition, though."

"Yeah?"

"If this blows up in our faces, then we pack up and get our asses back to Hampton immediately. If Danny does see family above all else, then us staying here any longer is a very risky proposition. If that happens, we turn all this over to some professionals and we are out of it, okay?"

Chloe nodded, knowing he always had their best interests at heart. But if it did backfire, she was still trying to come up with some way to protect Adam and Katie. She could not walk out on them if they were in danger as well. In all of this, the kids were just as innocent as Teresa had been. With that decision finally made, Harold and Chloe turned in for the night, both on pins and needles as to what might happen when they actually put this plan of Chloe's into action.

43

JULY 2008

*S*urprisingly, considering what they had talked about just before going to bed and how what lay ahead of them might have kept them tossing and turning, Harold and Chloe fell asleep quickly and into a dreamless rest. But a few hours later, they were abruptly wakened as their bed began to shake. Initially, it was just a mild tremor, much like what might be caused by the passing of a large vehicle nearby, but as the seconds ticked by, the tremors picked up in intensity, and the bed was soon trembling, and they grasped at the mattress for stability.

Coming out of a deep sleep, they both tried to understand what was happening and if it was real. As far as Harold knew, earthquakes were unheard of in South Carolina, but from descriptions he had heard of from areas prone to them, that was his initial assessment. Once he came to full consciousness, he threw back the covers and was about to grab Chloe and have them move to take cover under the frame of the bedroom door as he recalled reading that when you had to move quickly, that was a good spot to try to ride out the quakes if you did not have time to escape the structure you were in.

But as soon as he touched her on the arm, he followed her line of vision and joined her in what she was staring at across the bedroom. Small, multiple whirlwinds of air had formed and were visible only by the dust and loose debris they had sucked up in their funnels. It seemed utterly impossible as they had closed the windows earlier against a light rain that had begun to fall as they were turning in. But before either of them could make another move or figure out what the hell was going on, the small whirlwinds coalesced into one funnel that reached from the floor to just below the high ceiling. The bed had now stopped moving, but the new development seemed worse.

They both snapped their attention to the door as it swung slowly closed and latched firmly. Now completely freaked out, Chloe watched wild-eyed as Harold dove to the door and tried with all his strength to force it open. But it was as if the wood had swelled from humidity or otherwise frozen in place, and all his efforts were futile. He carefully made his way back to the bed and sat with Chloe as the whirlwind began to slow its revolutions, and instead of a funnel, the image of Teresa Thompson appeared once again before them. It was like the vortex had simply changed over into her human form, like it had been the way she traveled from place to place, Chloe thought.

The apparition, as before, said nothing to them, but

the look on her face was pained and pleading. Chloe felt the entity's eyes lock onto hers, and though she did not know how, she could feel the thing communicating with her without actually speaking. Had Teresa not appeared in such a plaintive and humble way, Chloe supposed she might have been terrified. With that in mind, she just relaxed and let the message from Teresa flow into her mind. Harold glanced toward her, unsure of what exactly was transpiring, but he detected that something unique was going on. The look on Chloe's face as she gently closed her eyes and breathed calmly made him think she was getting some message from Teresa just then.

He did not know if it was because she was a woman or because Teresa might know she had experienced a paranormal event before, but deep in his bones, he just knew that was what was happening. He sat quietly and waited. After a few minutes, the apparition of Teresa Thompson just devolved again before returning to the form of a calm whirlwind once more. The funnel slowed in intensity until it just collapsed in on itself and disintegrated as if it had never been there in the first place. Chloe opened her eyes and wiped away a tear. Harold had a pretty good idea of what she had been told, but he let Chloe tell him about the experience anyway as the whole thing had been incredible to observe from his vantage point.

"She talk to you?" Harold asked just as an opener.

Chloe nodded. "It was odd. I just kind of heard her voice in my head."

"And?" Harold prompted, though he already had a pretty good idea what it was.

Chloe exhaled and laid out what he had been expecting. Teresa desperately needed their help before her murder just went unsolved for good.

"She say who it was?"

Chloe shook her head. "Nope…just indicated that if we followed our instincts and were open to what assistance she could give us, that the guilty party would be revealed in perfect time and in a way that would leave no questions unanswered."

"Pretty cryptic," Harold replied.

"Either that or perhaps she didn't actually see who it was. Maybe she got attacked from behind or something. Or even more insidious, it might be that if it was Jonathan that she is still too tied to him emotionally to let herself admit it."

"But you still have the feeling it is Jonathan, right?"

"It is the only possibility that makes any sense to me with everything else we know. Some random killing by a transient intruder doesn't seem right."

"So you want to take a shot at solving this thing once and for all?"

Chloe nodded and looked at him seriously. "For the sake of everyone involved, yeah. My real fear now is that we may be too late."

"You think he might have everything in place and may be ready to head out soon if he has not fled already?"

She nodded again.

"Well…we're putting a lot of stock in the manifestations of Teresa Thompson, Chloe. But all my former skepticism is long gone after tonight. I still think it's pretty risky, but count me in. You still think that going through Danny is our best bet?"

"Unless you have a better idea, I don't see any other option if we really want to minimize any potential danger from Jonathan if he is our guy."

Harold shook his head. "I kind of feel fifty-fifty about that approach, but yeah, I don't see any other way. Let me give Danny a call and see if we can convince him that Jonathan might not be the truly grieving and anguished man he appears to be. And maybe pray we're not way off track here."

Chloe nodded and smiled grimly, knowing her plan could go either way. But with her lack of any real religious beliefs, she was counting more on having Teresa Thompson looking over them than any divine intervention to catch them if they fell. Knowing more sleep was not likely, Harold and Chloe sat down and jotted out an actual dialogue they thought had the best chance of being successful with Danny, taking into account any of several possibilities of how he might react. After a few hours of back-and-forth discussion and editing, they felt like they had a good approach. It was hardly bulletproof, they knew, but it was the best they could hope for. If Danny Thompson was really the man they thought he was, even the worst outcome, they were sure, would be minimal in terms of how vulnerable and exposed to danger they would be afterward if it all just blew up in their faces.

44

JULY 2008

*T*he timing of their plan to try to get Danny Thompson convinced that his brother might not be exactly who he thought he was and that there might be sufficient evidence to at least open an official investigation into Jonathan's involvement with Teresa's murder was fortuitous. It was Saturday, and Tony had given Harold and his guys the day off as he had a family commitment down in Savannah that would last through the weekend. It not only freed up some extra time for Harold to accompany Chloe for their meeting with Danny but also put Tony off-site just to avoid any complications from what might happen after they talked.

As well, Reggie had just finished up from his breakfast responsibilities and would not be back until mid-afternoon to begin putting dinner together. Harold found Chloe sitting alone in the dining room, still nursing her final cup of coffee from breakfast, when he walked over to join her.

"You get hold of Danny?" she asked as he sat.

"I did."

"Any problems so far?"

"Nope. I stayed right on our script and asked him if we could take him up on his kind, standing offer of help."

"He ask for any details?"

"Not specifically, but I could tell from his voice that he was curious, so I gave him just enough to get him to agree to meet."

"Like?"

"I just said that we were finding ourselves facing a serious situation regarding Jonathan and the estate, but this was a totally separate issue than what had almost caused us to leave a few weeks back."

"Well done, and he will meet with us today?"

"He will. I guess I twisted the truth a bit just to get him to say yes, but he could tell this was urgent."

"He coming by here?"

"No, actually he's in town, taking care of some legal stuff for one of his business partners and needs to run some other errands later up in Walterboro, so he suggested we meet at that café by the post office, Penelope's. You know it?"

"I've been by there but never inside."

"I think meeting him there instead of here is good—kind of neutral ground, emotionally speaking. Maybe not as private, but I'm sure we can find an isolated tale away from any prying ears."

"When?"

"He suggested 1 PM, and I said that would be fine."

Chloe nodded and finished her coffee. "You still with me on this, Harold?"

"Absolutely. Why don't we take a quick walk just to clear our minds and make sure we're in total agreement on our game plan."

* * *

THE STROLL through the woods was beneficial to both of them, and by the time they were driving into Green Pond, Harold and Chloe felt confident and prepared. They parked and went inside and saw Danny waiting for them while chatting with a young woman behind the register. He waved when he saw the couple and motioned for them to follow him toward the back of the café. He pushed open the screen door just ahead, and they all went to a small table on a nicely shaded patio.

"Penelope's can get busy on the weekends," Danny said as they sat. "I figured this was a better spot than somewhere inside with too many ears, you know?"

"Sure," Harold replied, "good idea."

"And I asked Kathy—the woman you saw me chatting with—to make sure we had some privacy unless they got overloaded and she had to send customers out here."

As if she had heard her name, Kathy showed up just then and took their order for lemonades. "Looks pretty quiet, Danny," when she brought them their drinks. "You should be fine out here."

"Thanks, Kath. I appreciate it."

"Maybe return the favor by taking me to lunch one day like you keep promising?" she said with a grin.

"You bet. I promise," Danny replied.

She wandered back inside, and Harold looked at Danny and smirked.

"You been reneging on lunch dates, Danny?"

He laughed. "No. Well, yeah, I guess so. Kathy and I have this…well, it's complicated."

Harold and Chloe chuckled with him and did not press him for anything more.

"So," Danny continued after taking a sip of his drink, "you sounded pretty urgent on the phone earlier. What's up?"

Harold looked to Chloe, and she nodded. It was her gig, so they agreed she would take the lead.

"Since we last spoke, Danny, we have come across a few unsettling things that we wanted to run by you and get your take on based on your generous offer to help if we needed it."

"Sure. Is this related to your discomfort from before?"

"Not really, " Chloe lied. "But we think you're the one who should know about this and then see if you think we're onto something or there's an ongoing situation that we're not aware of."

"But you said it had to do with Jonathan, right?"

"Yeah," she replied. "Since you know your brother better than anyone and might be privy to what he's involved in with his new business ventures, we wanted to talk to you before we stepped into something that's none of our business."

"Of course. You've got me curious now. What is this all about?"

Chloe took a long draw on her drink and then began to fill Danny in on what she had unearthed. Danny sat silent and seemingly stoic as Chloe told of having innocently overheard Jonathan on the phone with either an accountant or some financial advisor as to a strategy for consolidating some investments that would make them more liquid. He fidgeted slightly as she moved on to describe the disordered collection of what she considered sensitive financial documents on his desk that seemed to back up that phone conversation. She said it was like he had begun to act on whatever advice he had received on that call.

It was at that point that Chloe paused. She wanted Danny to have a few seconds to register that before she launched into having stumbled across Teresa's diary. From the beginning, she and Harold had decided not to bring up the visits from Teresa with Danny again, knowing how he felt about such things. They figured that putting any weight on how a ghost coming to them for help might add to their apprehensions was a waste of breath. And quite frankly, if they were in his shoes and someone came to them with such a story, they would find it ludicrous as well if they had not had the experiences seeing her that they had.

But the diary discovery, she was sure, would be the clincher if Danny was to take their concerns seriously. Chloe took a deep breath and went into as much detail as she thought was needed concerning what Teresa had secretly recorded about her life back then and her fear that her life might be in danger. Danny showed no reaction as she finished up, and she and Harold sat, waiting nervously to see just how he would respond and what would happen next.

45

JULY 2008

"Any chance you have that diary with you?" Danny asked quietly.

Chloe dug into the bag she was carrying and handed it over. "If you pick up her entries beginning about eight or nine months before it ends, just before her murder, you'll see what I described," Chloe said.

Danny thumbed over to where the pages went blank and then worked his way back as she had suggested and scanned that part while they waited.

"It's pretty rambling, Chloe," Danny finally said as he continued to read along.

"Yeah, I know. Did you know she was keeping this?"

"Nope...first time I have ever seen this or even heard of it."

"Sure seems like she felt like someone had it in for her, though," Harold added.

"In places," Danny agreed, "but interwoven among those concerns is a lot of...I don't even know how to describe what's here."

"Paranoia?" Chloe offered. "We both saw it that way, but in the end, maybe her apparent paranoia was justified to some degree. I mean, she did end up dead."

"To some degree," Danny replied, "but to me, it's even beyond that."

"Are you aware if Teresa might have been on any medication or if she ever had any mental health issues?" Harold asked, hoping to have Danny possibly clear up the way she had written near the end.

"Can't say as I do. From my experience, Teresa was one of the most centered and well-balanced people I had ever met. If she were being treated for anything, she kept it a close-guarded secret."

Chloe decided it was time to drop their bomb. "So, Danny, what we're really concerned about is what this looks like when you add it all up."

"Wanna give me a hint because I am not sure I see any connection... Hold on a second; I think I am seeing what you are getting at. Are you thinking Teresa was referring to Jonathan, and now with all this financial stuff, you think he might be cashing out to disappear in case he's finally found out?"

Chloe shrugged. "We know how you feel about Jonathan, Danny, but with all of this, you have to admit that it sure looks suspicious."

"Jonathan is just not capable of such a thing, guys. I know him," Danny said with great emotion. "And besides, I know he would never abandon Adam and Katie, not before Teresa was killed and certainly not now...just not an option."

"What about the sudden movement of all this

money into just several places?" Harold asked. "It does look like what was once perhaps more difficult to liquidate is now very available. You know anything about what he was doing in this new business of his?"

"Jonathan and I never talked much about our work with each other, just superficial stuff like guys do, you know?

Danny then went oddly quiet and sighed. Neither Harold nor Chloe could miss the growing sense of agitation and discomfort on his face and in his eyes. Chloe was uncertain if the reaction was because he actually knew more about the relationship between Jonathan and Teresa that might support the theory or if the whole revelation was just a complete shock to him and he was thinking it all over to see if he thought it might be possible...that maybe he did not know Jonathan as well as he thought he did.

Danny looked back down at the diary and seemed lost in the pages as if he were trying to reconcile the Teresa he had known with the utterly petrified version of her in the diary that seemed to be coming apart at the seams. Harold looked to Chloe and raised his eyebrows when the lack of further discussion seemed to be at a standstill. She nodded, and he picked up the mantle.

"Unless you have any other explanation or better suggestion, Danny, we just feel like we have no choice but to go the police with all of this and let some real professionals take over. Chloe and I are hardly qualified, and at some point, someone needs to speak directly to Jonathan and get his side. There may be a perfectly rational and reasonable explanation for all of it."

Danny said nothing, just kept flipping through the diary.

"It may be," Chloe interjected, "that he knew something about Teresa that none of us do, and it would explain these bizarre entries in the diary. And the money? Most of it is foreign to me. He may be setting up something completely innocent and benign with the fund transfers. But someone needs to ask some questions to find out the truth."

Danny nodded and closed the diary. "Yeah…" he finally croaked back. "It would kill me if you're right, but the truth needs to come out, if for no other reason than to protect Adam and Katie. I'm sure Jonathan could not do something like this in a million years. I would stake my own life on it, but I could never live with myself if I was wrong and Jonathan is not who I'm sure he is."

"Do you want to go with us to talk to them and explain that we might have a lead in the case for them after all this time?" Harold asked.

Danny tossed back the dregs of his lemonade which by that time was mostly melted ice.

"Tell you what, guys. How about this. Can you hold off on going to anyone official until I have a chance to speak to Jonathan myself face to face? You have uncovered a lot here—most of which has rocked me to the core. I'm sure Jonathan will tell me the truth if he is involved and it would save ruining his good name in Green Pond. I mean, what if Teresa was suffering from some mental disease and the ramblings in her diary were a result of that and nothing more. I know she doesn't name Jonathan specifically, but like yourselves, I'm sure detectives would make the same leap."

Harold and Chloe did not reply.

"I mean, I need to find out just how accurate all of this is—from the financial curiosities to whether or not Teresa might have been suffering from some condition none of the rest of us were aware of. It would be horribly unfair to just have him hauled into an interrogation with no warning. The news would spread like wildfire in this little town, and even if he's innocent, just having been a suspect would ruin his reputation.

"And what would it do to the kids? After all they've been through, even a justified suspicion by the police will likely set them back considerably, and maybe something they don't bounce back from this time."

Harold looked to Chloe, and she nodded slightly. It was what they had planned to do a while back but finally said no when the risk to them seemed too great. This would allow that now with Danny being the messenger.

"Look," Danny went on, "once again, I'm begging you to trust me. Let me talk to my brother, show him all you have come across, and get his explanation for it. I promise that once I get his version, incriminating or not, I will get back to you, and then we can involve the police if necessary. Fair enough?"

Ordinarily, Harold would have thought this not such a good idea, despite how forthcoming and open Danny had been with them. He was still not so sure that Danny might put Jonathan's freedom over the truth if he was guilty. For Danny, maybe blood was indeed thicker than water. But in the end, he went along with Chloe, and they agreed to let Danny handle the situation his way. They handed over Chloe's notes along with the diary and told Danny they would wait to hear back from him.

46

JULY 2008

*D*anny took off, and Harold and Chloe stayed behind to talk after he was gone.

"What do you think?" Harold asked. "Does Danny have a good chance to get to the bottom of this?"

"Truthfully? Right now, it feels like maybe a 70% chance at best," Chloe replied.

"You don't trust him to follow through on his promise?"

"Not that. I mean, with all we've seen of Danny so far, I think he'll absolutely dig into this."

"But?"

"We're putting a lot of faith into believing that Danny will be able to look beyond family if Jonathan is guilty."

"Did we just make a mistake turning over everything to him?"

"Hard to say, but what other option did we have? We obviously couldn't have gone directly to Jonathan, even if we could track him down since he never seems to be around. And I have this gut feeling that if we had gone to the police after this conversation with Danny —you know, saying we don't feel comfortable with him trying to talk to Jonathan first—that he might have tipped Jonathan off just out of loyalty to his brother. He might not be guilty, but letting him know a police inquiry was imminent might have pushed him to flee regardless."

"Just to avoid any investigation on him?"

"Exactly…"

"So, just looking at the worst outcome here, what if Jonathan is guilty? And Danny is aware of that…he could just toss the stuff we just handed over and give him the lead time he needs to get out of town and possibly out of the country. And if he's unaware, there's still the possibility that his dedication to Jonathan is too strong, and he might just ignore it all and then tell us there's nothing to be concerned about—make up some tall tale to explain what you found."

Chloe grinned.

"I say something funny?" Harold asked, perplexed.

"No. It's just that I already considered that possibility, and I made copies of everything just in case."

"You sly boots," Harold replied with a smile as he kissed her.

"So now we just wait, I guess, " Chloe said as she laid her head on his shoulder.

"I hate that, like some song I remember from way back. Not sure who it was, 'waiting is the hardest part….'"

* * *

Harold and Chloe took the kids on a picnic and spent the weekend relaxing and trying to put what was hanging over their heads out of their minds as much as they could. It was a nerve-racking few days, even though they knew there was not much more they could do until they heard back from Danny. They had done all they could, but Harold was extremely thankful that Chloe had been smart enough to prepare a backup set of evidence if it all blew up with Danny. Monday came and went, and still, they had heard nothing from Danny. Chloe made several calls to Danny's cell phone, but each time, all she got was his voice mail kicking in without it ringing, as if he had the thing turned off. She left messages, just asking him to get back to them to let them know what had transpired.

When Tuesday came to a close and they still had not heard anything from Danny, Harold and Chloe began to get worried.

"Think my worst-case scenario is playing out?" Harold asked her as they sat on the bed that night to decide what to do next.

"Though that's a definite possibility, I don't think so. Just call it my intuition, I guess. Danny just seems like he had enough character and decency to do the right thing, family ties aside."

"What other option is there, then?"

"Actually, one we had not considered previously, I think, and we should have, I guess."

"Oh?"

"Yeah," Chloe replied with a serious expression on her face. "Remember how we decided not to go to Jonathan directly in case he was Teresa's killer and it would put us in danger if he thought we were looking into it?"

"Yeah…so?"

"Well, what if that's what's happened to Danny? What if he went to his brother and laid out all the evidence, unaware that he was the killer, and Jonathan was so desperate that he turned on Danny. That might be another wild assumption, but I guess if Jonathan truly felt trapped and backed into a corner, that brother or not, he might do what he feels he has to do to escape."

"Fuck!" Harold exclaimed. "How did that one get by us?"

"No idea, but it sure would explain why we haven't heard back from Danny and why his phone seems out of commission. Even if he hadn't been able to get hold of Jonathan or if it was nothing, I'm sure we would've heard back from him."

Harold nodded and felt a sudden wave of guilt, as if they had inadvertently just put Danny's life in danger. But even worse, he realized they were now completely vulnerable if Jonathan was aware of what they had been up to. Their options for what was next had just been reduced to one, as far as Harold was concerned. They had to get out of Aberdeen Estates, and they had to go right now!

"Okay, Chloe," he said after a brief lag in their

conversation, "that's it. We've got to get out of here, and the sooner, the better."

"What about Adam and Katie?" she asked with a pained look on her face.

Harold sighed. "I know this is tough for you, Chloe, but I think we need to get away, alert some authorities, and then let them take over. It won't help Adam and Katie if we get killed. I promise you we'll do everything possible to get them out of here as well, but right now, we need to get ourselves to a safe place."

Chloe knew he was right, but it still made her horribly concerned that Jonathan might do something to the kids in the meantime or just snatch them up if he was taking off after Danny's confrontation with him. Everyone said he loved them more than anything, but if he was in panic mode now and feeling like he had no other way out, she did not discount them becoming collateral damage in his scheme.

"Okay, but let's move fast in case we can get someone to come back with us and get those kids out safely."

"Deal. Grab the copies of all the evidence while I pack our stuff. We'll go straight to the police and show them everything, explaining that time is of the essence as we feel Jonathan's plan to flee the country may be near, if it hadn't happened already. And also, that the welfare of two children may be at risk."

She nodded and dashed off to collect the reams of paper she had stashed away that had her notes as well as appliable sections of Teresa's secret diary. While she was busy gathering what they knew was vital to alerting the authorities to what they suspected Jonathan was behind—and now possibly including the unknown whereabouts of his brother who had gone to confront him about Teresa's death—Harold tossed their empty bags onto the bed. Without concern about whose things went into which bag, he stuffed clothes and other personal items away as fast as possible. When one suitcase was full, he shut it and began on the other.

Fortunately, they had not brought a lot of stuff with them, as just a few minutes after Chloe returned with a thick folder of copies of the documents, Harold was latching the second bag. They both began to make one last frantic run through the room, making sure they had everything when the late afternoon skies turned dark and heavy with clouds and it began to look more like night outside. Harold felt a stab of anxiety as a massive clap of thunder struck and a vicious, jagged shard of lightning ripped over the nearby wood lightning the whole property harshly. Without another second's delay, rain began to pour from the clouds. It was like all had been fine one second, and the next, some huge overhead faucet had been flipped on full blast.

They both stopped in their tracks and froze. They had never seen rain like this before in their lives.

"Think we can make a run for it?" Chloe asked with hesitation in her voice, as the visibility just outside the window was maybe only a few feet at best.

"It can only get worse. Let's go!"

But just then, both Adam and Katie came bursting

in on them as another explosion of thunder shook the house and a snaking arc of lightning shot downward and connected with one of the largest trees nearby. It was like a bomb going off, and the tree fell across the only road leading away from Aberdeen Estates. With Adam and Katie clinging to them as they trembled with fear, Harold looked at Chloe, and she did not like what she saw in his eyes.

"Now what?" Chloe asked quietly as they tried to comfort the kids.

47

JULY 2008

$\mathcal{A}$fter breakfast that morning, Reggie had come down with a fever and had left for the day. Chloe had told him she would be able to take care of dinner that night so he could rest and recover. As well, Tony and his guys had been away all day at another project while he waited on some materials he had ordered for the work at the mansion to arrive. Harold and Chloe were on their own, with no one to call on for help. Even a cell phone call at this point seemed futile since the road was blocked and the rain was too torrential for anyone to hazard a trip out to them.

"Seems like our options have just been narrowed for us, I guess," Harold replied. "The storm is just too dangerous to try to travel in, and with that tree blocking the road, the storm kind of becomes a moot point."

"And we sure cannot take off and just leave the kids on their own," Chloe added.

Harold nodded. "Despite the urgency of our situation, I guess we wait out this storm. Once things stop or at least calm down enough, I can go out there and see about clearing the road. Maybe there's enough space to just squeeze around the tree, and if not, it will be chain saw time."

"What if Jonathan is on his way back to deal with us after talking to Danny?"

Harold shrugged. "I guess we just have to be on guard and do the best we can. Right now, there's not much else we can do until there's some reasonable and safe way to get out of here. Even taking Adam and Katie with us and making a mad dash seems rash and foolhardy to me. All four of us might get killed by the storm in the process."

"What if we have to stay overnight?"

"If we do, we'll just have to make the best of it and hope that maybe the storm and the damaged tree will prevent Jonathan from getting back here as well."

They turned their attention to Adam and Katie and did their best to reassure and calm them as the storm continued to rage. Chloe could see the anxiety in their little eyes, but each minute that went by seemed to bring them a little less agitation. At least, Chloe thought, their fear was just based on the storm itself. They had no idea what else was in the works at the moment and what other danger might lurk for them from their father's hidden scheme.

"Maybe get them some dinner and then do something to distract them from the storm?" Chloe suggested.

"Good for us as well," Harold replied.

But just as they stood to walk the kids downstairs to put together some food and then suggest a game or two to pass the time, another bolt of lightning streaked across the dark sky, and the power in the mansion instantly went dead. The lights in the bedroom that they had flipped on when the skies clouded over went out, and the room was almost as dark as if it was the middle of the night. Adam and Katie both screamed and clung tighter to Harold and Katie, having lost all the progress they had made just moments ago in calming down. They could feel the tremors from the kids' bodies shake against them once again.

"Of course, I guess it was just a matter of time," Harold muttered with unwilling resignation.

"It's okay, kids," Chloe said soothingly as she rubbed Katie's back. "The lightning probably just made the fuses short-circuit." She looked to Harold.

"Yeah," he replied as he gave Adam a quick hug, "it happens all the time in electrical storms. Let me go check the breaker box, and if it is not that, then we'll just light some candles and wait on the power company in Green Pond to get it all fixed."

Adam and Katie smiled weakly but did not loosen their grip on Harold and Chloe.

"Chloe," Harold continued, "why don't you look around for some candles while I run down to the breaker box to see if we just need a simple reset."

She nodded as Harold guided Adam, with the boy's stubborn reluctance to release his hold, over to Chloe and his sister, who were sitting on the bed. But before Harold could get around the end of the mattress to grab his flashlight and head down to see if he could get the lights back on, he froze as he spotted a wavering glow leaking on and off under the closed bedroom door. It seemed to be coming from down the hallway toward them. It was not a strong light, but it was getting more visible as it got closer. He got Chloe's attention, and she looked to the space underneath the door. All she could think of was that Teresa had come to see them once again.

"Teresa?" Chloe whispered over to Harold as he stood unmoving, and he nodded in return.

Had Adam and Katie not been visited by their mother already, Chloe might have been frantic about dealing with Teresa's sudden appearance. But all things considered, it seemed like a hand out to help them at last. The other positive detail that occurred to her was that it was likely Teresa would come to them in her most recent mode, that of pleading and kindness rather than some presence to scare and intimidate as she had appeared when they had first encountered her.

The light continued to gain strength and seep more and more through the gap, and both Harold and Chloe relaxed, sure Teresa had come to their aid. Then the knob turned, slowly unlatching the door, and Chloe felt a tinge of unease. *Why would a ghost need to use the doorknob?* she asked herself. *Wouldn't she just come through the solid wall? Or why not just show up in the room like she last time? Something is not quite right.*

Suddenly, the door burst open and banged against the wall inside the bedroom with the force of its movement. They both looked up in horror and sudden panic, wishing with all their hearts that what they saw now *was* Teresa Thompson. Instead, they found themselves face to face with the imposing and towering figure of Jonathan Thompson. He was holding a flashlight, which had been causing the growing light they had thought was part of Teresa's manifestation.

He looked wild-eyed and was panting from exertion as he stared at them, water running in constant rivulets from his head and shoulders. Fortunately, he did not seem to be holding a weapon of any kind at the moment, but the look on his face and the timing of his appearance just now made that piece seem inconsequential.

48

JULY 2008

*C*hloe was scared for herself and Harold, but at the same time, she was even more concerned for Adam and Katie. *Will Jonathan be so callous and cold and single-minded in his nefarious plan as to include his children in whatever he has in store for her and Harold?* With what she had heard about the man, it seemed utterly impossible. But looking into his desperate eyes just now, Chloe felt all bets might be off. He said nothing, though; he just stood and stared at them as he shivered from the chill of having come through the downpour. The dead, empty glaze of his glare sent daggers into Chloe's heart as she feared his desperation and perhaps that he saw himself as a man with no way out or any other options would have risked coming through such a dangerous storm to write the final chapter.

Chloe got Adam and Katie to their feet and positioned herself in front of them as a rough human shield, though she knew it was unlikely to be of any use if Jonathan flew into action here. It was more of an instinctive response, she guessed, more than a barrier. Harold stepped back to make sure he kept between Jonathan and Chloe and the kids. But it was like he could not see his children at all…as if they were invisible as his eyes panned back and forth between Harold and Chloe without moving his head. Her only hope at that point was that he would take her and Harold away and not kill them in front of Adam and Katie, though that was not of much solace regarding her own life. If she were going down, Chloe promised herself, right then and there, that she would go down swinging and that Adam and Katie would stay safe if she could figure out how to make it happen.

She chanced a quick glance at Harold, wondering if she would pick up any nonverbal clues from him as to any possible way out of this predicament. But he looked just as hopeless and trapped as she felt. If only there were another way out of the bedroom so they could at least try to make a run for it. That in and of itself would likely just delay the inevitable, as Jonathan would know the layout far better than they did, but at least it would be a possibility. But all that lay behind them was the door to the bathroom, which went nowhere. In fact, there was not even a window in the room to try to squeeze out of after dashing in there and locking the door behind them. Chloe was never one to give up, no matter how bad things seemed, but just then, she was beginning to resign herself to the situation.

She and Harold had gotten themselves immersed in a

situation they should have either just walked away from or alerted the police to long ago, but they had felt sure working with Danny that all would be fine. And now it looked as if they might be responsible for Danny's death. *And then what about the kids?* Chloe would do what she could, but things did not look good for anyone just then. Her heart sank. As hard as they had tried and as much care and precaution as they had taken, Jonathan had sidestepped it all and outwitted them. Now she and Harold were about to be added to the list of his victims.

Harold began to step back toward Chloe as a very menacing-looking Jonathan Thompson moved closer. It was like some macabre dance between the two of them as Jonathan kept pace with Harold's retreat. For the first time, Jonathan, still struggling to catch his breath and dripping all over the floor from the storm, looked to them and spoke.

"Listen to me," he choked out, his breath still short as he held out a hand, "you have to come with me… now! All of you!"

Sure that this was how they would die, Chloe stood her ground, just off Harold's shoulder as she continued to shield the kids.

"It is a matter of life and death, guys!" Jonathan went on with great urgency. "Every minute counts!"

His expression had softened a bit, but Chloe still did not trust the words coming out of his mouth. The cold and empty, vacant stare had melted away as well, but sure that he was a master at deception, neither Harold nor Chloe made a move toward him, nor did they let him get in a position so he could grab Adam or Katie. Harold slyly maneuvered himself as close as he could get to Chloe as he could without actually standing on her toes and whispered to her out of the side of his mouth while never taking his eyes away from Jonathan's laser stare at them.

"You trust me, right?" he whispered.

"Of course.." Chloe replied.

"No matter how crazy?"

"Yeah, yeah…what?" she shot back in frustration.

"Okay…on three, I'm going to grab your arm. Make sure you have a tight hold on the kids or at least can push them along. Ready?"

Chloe nodded, hoping Jonathan would not suddenly reach out to snag them and that Harold had some trick up his sleeve that she was unaware of.

"One…two…three!" Harold exclaimed as he moved with cat-like quickness to the side and pulled Chloe with him as the four of them dove toward the open bathroom door.

"No! Wait!" Jonathan cried out as he flailed just a second too late and the heavy bathroom door slammed in his face.

He pounded on the door in vain, but all Harold and Chloe felt was that they had just barely escaped the dame fate that both Teresa and Danny had met, at least temporarily. They stood with their backs to the door as Jonathan pounded away and yelled for them to listen to him and open the door before it was too late. Adam and Katie were wild-eyed and scared, having no idea why Harold and Chloe had yanked them away from their father like they had.

"It's okay, kids," Chloe said as she saw their confused little faces. "Your dad is not well right now, and we need to get you to a safe place so we can get someone to make him better."

They were not completely convinced, she saw, but they nodded anyway, relying on the trust and bond they had developed with Chloe since she had come to take care of them. Then she looked to Harold, wondering what the hell he had in mind bringing them into a room with no means of escape.

"I do trust you, Harold, but what now? I thought of this earlier, but there's no way out of here except back through the bedroom, not even a window. It might delay the inevitable, but sooner or later, that maniac out there is going to be able to break down the door."

"He's a persistent little bugger, eh?" Harold said with a grin that made Chloe wonder if he had lost his mind.

"Hardly the time for jokes, Harold," she replied, feeling a sudden sense of doom.

"I couldn't agree more. However, what you don't know is what I do based on my work here with Tony."

"Huh?"

"Follow me."

Chloe corralled the kids and followed Harold as he walked to the oversized storage closet between the sink and the bathtub. He opened the door and then disassembled the shelves inside after removing all the stuff that had been on them. She watched him with growing curiosity but was still quite baffled as to what he was up to. Harold bent down and slid inside the closet on his knees and reached out to slid back a panel that had been painted to blend in with the wall around it. Chloe had not even noticed it. The opening was not huge but certainly large enough for the average person to enter.

"Any claustrophobia?" Harold asked Chloe quietly so the kids would not hear.

"No more than the average person, I suppose," Chloe replied, though tight and enclosed spaces were not exactly on her list of fun places to be. "What is this thing?"

"When Tony and I were putting in some electrical wiring and some tricky plumbing pipes for the bathrooms up here, we thought it might be a good idea to put in a little extra crawlspace to make it easier to do repairs if needed."

"Jonathan know about this?"

"It is possible, I suppose. I have no idea how much or how little Tony has made him aware of, but as much as he has been away on business, I seriously doubt it."

"And it comes out where?"

"The ductwork peels off the crawlspace after just a few feet and then feeds on an angle down to the kitchen, maybe a few hundred feet in all."

"You think it's too dangerous for them?" she asked as she motioned to Adam and Katie with her head.

"You kidding? Watch this. You kids up for an adventure?" Harold asked as Adam and Katie moved closer to take a look.

He breathed a sigh of relief when they both nodded

vigorously and smiled. It was one of many great things about kids, Harold thought. They seem to be able to live in the moment much more than when you reached his age. The scene with Jonathan seemed long-forgotten already, and they looked on this as a game of some sort, he figured.

"Great, just think of this as a mysterious cave you are the first ones to have found. You will have a great story to tell everyone when they want to hear about your brave and adventurous exploits!"

That made Adam and Katie smile wider, but Chloe was certainly somewhat less confident than them.

"Just to make sure you get in safely, I'll go first and then lower you down, and we can go exploring, okay?"

They nodded, and Harold looked at Chloe one last time as the muffled sounds of Jonathan at the door continued as he was pleading with them to come back before it was too late. She was impressed with how he had distracted the kids from their predicament and made the whole thing feel like just another game. She just wished she felt more at ease with this plan. Harold saw the anxiety on her face.

"Chloe? You okay?" Harold asked as she appeared to be miles away at the moment.

"Yeah, sure. Going back is certainly no option, so let's get moving. We need to get out and then get help before he tracks us down."

Harold nodded and levered himself through the opening and reached up to help first Adam and then Katie through and onto the crawlspace floor. He looked up and saw Chloe kneeling hesitantly at the aperture.

"This will work, Chloe. I promise. Just back in, I will help you down, but close that panel as best you can on your way, okay?"

She nodded and did as he said, and the four of them were plunged into complete darkness. The panel slid back as if on rollers, and she hoped if Jonathan managed to get inside the bathroom, he would not see it. The disassembled shelves and their contents were something they could do nothing about, but maybe, just maybe, it would take him enough time to figure out how they had escaped before he came after them. She clicked on her penlight and panned the beam to check on everyone.

"You okay, kids?" she asked.

They nodded, still smiling as if this were just some great game they got to play with Harold and Chloe. She handed Harold the light so he could lead them out.

"Everyone grab hold of the person in front of you, okay? Lead on, Great White Hunter," she said as she fell in behind Adam and Katie as Harold moved them carefully to the declined section of ductwork he had described.

49

JULY 2008

$\mathscr{C}$hloe's penlight bounced slightly in Harold's hand as they moved through the crawlspace. Both Adam and Katie were able to stand while Harold and Chloe had to bend over uncomfortably to avoid the low ceiling. They could still hear Jonathan's voice leaking down from the locked bathroom door as well as his continued pounding against it, but it was getting less and less audible as they moved along. It seemed to Chloe that he would eventually realize they were not coming out, but maybe he would be persistent enough to keep at it to give them some lead time to make their escape. She felt her stomach pitch and roll with nerves, praying Harold's plan was going to work. As for the kids? Well...they seemed unaffected, as if it was all just a great adventure as Harold had convinced them it would be.

After another few minutes, Harold came to a stop, and they stood just behind him as the beam of light reflected off some shiny metal ductwork and then a dark maw below. Jonathan's pounding and yelling had faded to nothing, and they were not sure if that meant he had finally given up or if they had just moved out of range to be able to hear him. To Chloe, the latter seemed unlikely, with the former meaning he might be elsewhere in the mansion now on the hunt for them. That made her shiver slightly with anxiety. Harold looked back at Adam and Katie.

"Okay, kids, ready for some fun?"

Chloe was amazed at how he could make this whole thing seem like some innocuous outing to keep them distracted from the reality of what they might be facing when they got out of the space behind the walls. And amazingly, he was ready when they looked into the black hole and suddenly had expressions of uncertainty for the first time since they had slipped through the panel in the bathroom closet.

"It's just like that slide out in the yard that you guys play on all the time. Only this one isn't as steep. I'll go first to show you how easy it is. Once I'm down, I'll shine the light up so you can see and then catch you when you come down. Ready?"

There was a mixture of trust and hesitation on their faces as Harold explained the situation, but eventually, they just nodded as Harold sat at the edge of the incline and pushed off, disappearing into the dark. There was a soft thump as he came to a stop at the bottom, and he aimed the light back up toward them.

"See how easy?" he said. "One at a time, now…you'll love it!"

They looked back to Chloe, and she nodded and

forced herself to smile though her real thoughts were on what would happen once they were down. Adam went first and slid along the slick duct until he shot into Harold's waiting arms.

"Wow!" he exclaimed as Harold helped him up. "That was fun!"

"Okay, Katie," Harold said, "your turn."

After watching her brother go down with such ease and lack of fear, Katie followed suit. They were both bubbling and giggling after she arrived with Harold and Adam. Chloe then sat on the lip and joined them right away. They linked up again as they had before, and Harold led them along a narrow passageway where all four of them could stand up. He motioned to the kids to be as quiet as possible as he did not want to give away their position in case Jonathan had given up his quest at the bathroom door and was now close by and might hear them. He got them to stop after another few feet, dropped to his stomach, and began to crawl through an opening just large enough to allow an adult with a few inches to spare.

Harold slid open another panel and carefully peered in all directions before finally emerging in the kitchen. He looked around quickly, and when he was sure Jonathan was nowhere to be found, he went back to the open panel.

"Okay, guys, the coast is clear! Come on out, one at a time, but don't tarry."

They followed his orders, and Adam, then Katie, and finally Chloe crawled out of the narrow slot and joined Harold in the kitchen as he slid the panel back into place silently.

"Can we go again?" Adam asked with a smile.

Harold chuckled. "Maybe later, pal. Right now, we need to get away and get help for your father, remember?"

Adam nodded as if he had completely forgotten why they had gone on this route, to begin with. It was still dark out as Harold glanced at his watch and saw it was still late. Fortunately, the storm from the night seemed to have tapered to just a light shower, and the winds had fallen off. But the sun was still a few hours away from rising, so he kept the light on as they crept quietly but steadily through the kitchen and toward the back door. Harold was sure they had managed to evade Jonathan by using this unknown escape hatch only he and Tony were aware of, but still, he was on high alert as his pulse pounded in his ears since that was only his best guess.

He opened the door and began to lead them out onto the small porch behind the kitchen when his heart felt like it stopped. Chloe and the kids crowded behind Harold as he stood still, and Chloe gasped in shock and surprise. Standing in the doorway of the porch that led outside was Jonathan Thompson. Chloe was not sure if she felt like crying or cursing some unseen fate that had yet again turned against them. After all of that, they were trapped. It was all over.

Jonathan reached toward Harold as he stiffened. Chloe figured she had to at least put up some sort of fight against the murderous man. His expression was one of desperation and determination, and she had never been so scared in her life.

"Please don't hurt the children!" Chloe cried out as Jonathan reached toward them.

Jonathan stopped abruptly, and a quizzical look of confusion came over his face. "Huh?" he finally uttered. "What are you—"

And those were the last words that Jonathan Thompson ever spoke. Harold and Chloe watched in horror as Jonathan cried out in agony as the top of his head exploded in a spray of blood and gore, and he fell to the floor in a heap. They looked up to find themselves facing Danny Thompson, holding a shotgun that was still smoking as he stood just behind the now-dead body of his brother.

50

JULY 2008

$\mathcal{A}$fter they got over the shock of Danny having just saved them from the killing hand of Jonathan, it suddenly dawned on Harold and Chloe that Jonathan had not killed Danny after all. They had no idea why he had been so out of touch since their last conversation, but his timing could not have been more fortuitous. One more minute, Chloe figured, and both she and Harold and maybe Adam and Katie might have been killed as well.

"Danny," Chloe exclaimed as she smiled with great relief, "thank God you're here!"

"Yeah," Harold replied as he relaxed, "you just saved us. How can we ever thank you?"

Danny did not reply but just bent down to make sure Jonathan was indeed dead, though with how brutally he had been shot, Chloe could not imagine he could possibly have survived Danny's blast.

"What happened to you? Where have you been?"

Chloe asked as Danny stood and wiped Jonathan's blood that was on his hand on his pants.

"Oh...just here and there," Danny replied with a grin. "Sorry about being so lax in my communication."

Chloe stood with one arm around Adam and Katie as Danny straightened up to respond to her, but something in his eyes did not look right. Suddenly, without warning, he raised the stock of the shotgun and slammed it into the side of Harold's head, knocking him unconscious. Chloe could not believe her eyes as she realized they had been played all along. It had never been Jonathan at all—Danny was responsible for everything. Adam and Katie stood frozen in place as well, their brains trying to comprehend why their Uncle Danny had just shot their father and then attacked Harold. Chloe just reacted on instinct without regard to her own safety.

"Run, kids!" she screamed as she shoved them away from the advancing Danny Thompson. "Run as fast as you can and hide!"

They took off at top speed as Danny fell onto Chloe and jammed a chloroform-saturated rag across her mouth. She fought against him, but he was too strong and his vise-like grip was impossible to get free from. As unconsciousness began to take her over, Chloe looked down the hallway as Adam and Katie fled, screaming in terror. She glanced down to see the motionless body of Harold at her feet as the effects of the chloroform began to act and felt as if her world had just fallen apart. Black spots began to form in her vision until they all seemed to condense into one huge cloud and her eyes closed for good.

* * *

MUCH LATER, Chloe began to come to, but she felt as if she were being bounced around. It made no sense as her clouded brain was still trying to push away the effects of having been drugged. She could not move her arms, and her legs seemed useless as well, though, in her present state of mind, she was not sure if that was from them having been injured or just that her brain was not quite yet communicating with her muscles. Her mind kept saying stand up and move, but her muscles just did not seem to be getting the memo. With no other option, she gave up the struggle and sank back as the bouncing and jostling continued making her feel like she was being hauled around like a sack of potatoes. She exhaled and waited a few more minutes, and then suddenly, her head began to clear, and she got a better idea of her circumstances.

But that realization was even more terrifying than not knowing once she scanned her immediate surroundings. The bruises she had developed on her rear and back were from the cart she seemed to be an unwilling passenger in, and the journey was over some rough and rutted ground, thus the harsh ride. Her limbs were not dysfunctional nor necessarily being uncooperative with her brain—she was bound and gagged. Along with her in the cart were Harold, as well as Adam and Katie. Like herself, they were similarly restrained. She twisted her head to the right as far as she could and saw Danny driving an aging ATV that towed the cart over a horribly pitted dirt road snaking its way through some thick trees.

Harold was just coming around as well, but Chloe had no idea how long they had been out. The sun was up, and the ground was wet with pools of water in all of the ruts and potholes they were now bouncing through. There was a long trail of blood running down the side of his face and over his shirt and pants, but as far as she could tell, Harold was otherwise okay. Before she had passed out, she had feared the blow Danny had delivered might have killed him. The force likely had left him with a concussion at the least, but it was a relief to see him conscious and breathing. She would deal with his actual medical condition if and when she figured a way out of this new predicament. Chances were this was now all on her if Harold was too incapacitated to function properly from his injury.

And to add to her anxiety over her situation, she looked across the cart to see both Adam and Katie similarly bound and gagged. They were both crying and had looks of utter panic and terror in their eyes. Chloe wished she could go to them and tell them it would all be okay, but since she was not so sure of that herself, she was glad she did not have the option of lying to children. She recalled a book she had read once. The main character's mantra was "do not lie to the dog," a reference to regarding his beloved partner above all else. People he could live with lying to but not his dog.

That was how Chloe now felt concerning the kids. So with her only available option, she tried to communicate that she would make sure nothing happened to them with her eyes. She had no idea if that would end up being true or not, but she would surely give it her best shot. Chloe had always thought of herself as an excellent judge of human character and what was in a person's heart, but now she wondered. *How did she* and *Harold misread and misjudge Danny Thompson so thoroughly?* She pondered that as Danny slowed the ATV to maneuver around some fallen tree limbs and a very deep pool of water. There were no easy or definitive answers coming to her, but most likely, it was a combination of the rumors from the town from Roger Yardley and his crew, combined with what Reggie had told them, and how closed-off and cold Jonathan had appeared to them.

One thing was for sure, Danny Thompson was a master con artist and king of deception. For it was in the end that she and Harold had believed every word out of his mouth. Every time they had had a concern or fear that seemed to point to Jonathan and the gossip from town, Danny had stepped in to convince them it was impossible. His message was true, but it was just to make himself look as if he was their best friend and their only buffer of security between them and his brother. *But why?* That was what was baffling Chloe just now. *Did Danny kill Teresa, or did Jonathan do it with Danny's knowledge and possible help?*

But the more she thought all the possibilities over in her mind, the one that seemed to ring true for Chloe was that it had been Danny himself. Somehow Jonathan had found out and had come to rescue them during the storm. His insistence that they come with him before it was too late had not been an attempt to kill them but to get them to safety before Danny arrived on the scene. Had she and Harold not had such a skewed and biased view of Jonathan, they all might now be safe and sound, but there was nothing she could do about that decision at that point. *But why drag them all out in the woods to do away with them?*

Maybe Danny thought it would be too hard to dispose of multiple bodies or explain it all to anyone who came looking for them when they did not check in with Madeline Emery in Hampton. Harold had been speaking to her regularly in his absence. No one was likely to come looking for the kids as they were home-schooled, but surely Reggie and Tony would ask questions. *What is Danny's plan to deal with them?* The only thing that made sense to Chloe at the moment was that he planned on doubling back to the mansion to thoroughly dispose of Jonathan's body—if he had not done so already—and then just say he had arrived to find the place abandoned.

A story of Jonathan having taken the kids and left the bad memories of Aberdeen Estates behind might fly. He could concoct a tale whereby his brother had left him in charge to handle the mansion as he saw fit while he and the kids started over somewhere far away. He could then easily say he had wrapped up Harold and Chloe's involvement at the mansion and that the last he knew, they had returned to Hampton. With no signs of foul play, it was unlikely that anyone would question Danny's story. *But explaining a pile of dead bodies, including two small children on the mansion's grounds?* Even that one seemed impossible to survive, Chloe thought. All of that was well and good empirically, but that did nothing to provide her with a means to extract herself, Harold, and the kids before it was too late.

51

JULY 2008

*C*hloe wondered if he had been preparing for this ever since they had last spoken to him at Penelope's. *Seeing the noose tightening around his neck, did Danny decided to take more proactive action to protect himself? Maybe he has found an old sinkhole or some cavern opening where he plans to dispose of them. Or then again, maybe he is just going to dump them deep in the woods and let nature take care of them?* The forest here was very dense and heavy, and Chloe figured they had been traveling for quite a while, so it might well be that no one would discover their bodies for a very long time. And if and when they did, Danny Thompson would likely be long gone. He would be the one who had fled the country, not his brother.

Danny gunned the ATV a bit to get up a slight rise in the road and then pulled over in a small clearing and killed the engine. Chloe trembled, knowing she was about to get an answer to that question very soon. *There has to be some way out of this, but how?* Chloe continued to struggle against her restraints, as had Harold, but all they had managed to do was rub their skin raw, leaving bloody scrapes on their wrists. Danny walked to the rear of the cart and lowered the tailgate by releasing two cotter pins, one on each side of the cart. Chloe looked up at him, and what she saw now chilled her to the bone.

The Danny Thompson she thought they knew—kind, warm, empathetic, and always willing to lend a hand—was nowhere to be found. The man who bore his gaze into her now was foreign to her. Much like her initial impressions of Jonathan, Chloe saw only a cold and calculating sociopath with no concern for anyone. His once welcoming and caring expression had been replaced with the look of...well, it was like what Chloe had heard marine biologists described when telling of looking into the eyes of a shark—just black and blank and empty. In books and movies, Chloe had been aware of characters who could change their personalities like a chameleon on changing terrain, but this was her first actual experience with that.

Danny slipped a knife from his jeans and snapped open the blade. Chloe closed her eyes as she braced herself for the pain. But she gasped in relief when all Danny did was cut away her gag before going and doing the same for Harold. She worked her jaw muscles to loosen up the cramping she had felt from the gag. Harold did the same, but as Chloe feared, he still looked a bit out of it as she hazarded a glance his way. He was awake but just seemed disoriented and confused, surely suffering a concussion or worse, she assumed.

"What about the kids?" Chloe asked as Danny sat on the edge of the cart and gloated.

"I think not. We're way out in the woods here, but I don't trust these two little fuckers to keep their yaps shut. Little shrill voices can really carry. I figure you and Harold know better, though I don't think Harold is in any shape to say anything at the moment, assuming he even knows where or who he is."

So much for the loving-uncle façade, Chloe thought to herself as her blood boiled when Danny joked about what he had done to Harold. But with great effort, she tamped down her anger, knowing it would accomplish nothing to lash out at him.

"So now what, Danny?" she asked.

"I'm not sure. I mean, I'm still basking in just how easy it was to scam you, two idiots, into believing Jonathan had anything to do with Teresa's death. I told you he wasn't capable of such a thing, didn't I? But you couldn't let it go after hearing the stories from those yahoos in Green Pond, could you? It's not often that you come across such gullible foils in your life, Chloe. It's a shame to have to say goodbye to such easy marks."

Chloe knew he was trying to goad her into something foolish, though as she was still bound at the wrists and ankles, she had no idea what in the hell he thought she was going to do. Then she had a thought. Maybe a little psychological warfare might work. It was a long shot, she knew, but now that Danny had fully disclosed and revealed his genuine narcissistic and sociopathic personality, maybe getting him to talk and boast about his exploits might delay their fate long enough to give her another idea for an escape.

And one thing she saw now was that Danny Thompson loved to talk. And his favorite topic appeared to be Danny Thompson. If she could get him talking about what had really happened, it might give them a chance—slim as that might be—to survive. She would play to his ego and hope for the best.

"Why, Danny?" Chloe asked.

He laughed. "Yeah, I'm sure that question has been killing you—no pun intended based on what's coming your way soon. I guess the least I can do is fill in the blanks for you and hubby before the end. You both seem like decent and trusting people, not stupid...and that's your Achille's heel. During the ride out here, I'm sure you came up with some scenario to explain it all. Like I said, you're not a stupid woman, Chloe. And I'm also sure some of what you concluded is right on the money, but I don't think you have any idea just how simple the whole thing was. That's the trouble with you intellectuals, Chloe. You try to make things way more complicated than they need be."

"So enlighten me," Chloe replied with as little emotion in her voice as she could muster.

"You bet. My pleasure. Let me ask you this, Chloe. You seem like a woman who likes a good mystery. I mean, you couldn't let this one go, is that right?"

"I would say so. Why?"

"Well, my guess is all you really know about murder and mystery and intrigue comes from TV and the movies, maybe a novel or two. Would that be accurate?"

Chloe felt her ire rising again at his condescending manner, but she shrugged it off as just part of who Danny really was. "I guess. You had a question?" she asked with a tinge of impatience creeping into her delivery.

"Calm down, Chloe. I didn't mean anything by that. Just setting the stage. So what would you say are the two most prominent motives for a major crime—take murder, for example, since that's what we're talking about here?"

"Money and sex, I guess."

"Very good. And you were convinced that Jonathan was fleeing the country by liquidating his investments before anyone linked him to Teresa's murder. Which you thought might have been promoted by some sexual dalliance on her part that made him jealous enough to kill her."

She and Harold had never come to any conclusions about why Jonathan might have killed Teresa, but right now, she just wanted to keep Danny talking, so she just let him believe what he wanted to keep him engaged. The longer he droned on, the longer she stayed alive.

"Okay…"

"Well, the real story is so much simpler, my dear. You see, it never had anything to do with money from the beginning. It was always about sex." Danny stopped there to let her try to connect some dots on her own.

"You and Teresa?" Chloe finally asked.

"Ah…and the last horse finally crosses the finish line, eh, Chloe?"

His admission about that stunned her, but Chloe did not let on, not wanting him to have the satisfaction. She also wanted him to elaborate to draw this out as long as possible to try to give her time to come up with an escape strategy.

"I can see from your face that you did not see *that* one coming, so let me lay it all out for you." Danny continued as he stretched his legs in front of him, indicating a long story coming.

52

JULY 2008

"You see, Chloe," Danny began, "Jonathan and I were always close long ago just as I told you and Harold. But it was not my leaving the country for my own business ventures that caused a long and distant relationship between us. It was Teresa Faraday. Faraday was her maiden name. Once she came along, everything between us changed. As I'm sure you have seen from the newspaper articles and whatever else you decided to stick your nose into over her murder, Teresa was a beautiful woman. But her beauty went far beyond skin deep."

He looked away for a moment as if he were recalling old memories from before she had died. Chloe shuddered a bit as glimpses of the old Danny he had shown them earlier seemed to flash across his face as he thought back. That was just as creepy to her as his transformation into what he really was.

"Teresa was kind and generous, and...well, you get the idea. Anyway, when she and Jonathan began to see each other, it was like I got put into some box or just shoved aside. Perhaps you have had a friend somewhere in your life who pushed you aside once a romantic relationship became more important to them than your friendship?"

Chloe had not, but she just nodded as if she knew what he meant to keep him talking.

"And at one time, Jonathan and I were best friends, as well as brothers. It was painful to endure on several levels."

Chloe began to see where this was going. "You wanted her as well?" Chloe asked.

Danny nodded and sighed. "But she only had eyes for Jonathan, I'm afraid," he went on. "I kept hoping something might be awry between them since Jonathan's track record with women in lasting relationships was not good. But the longer they were together, the stronger their bond seemed to be growing. The whole situation began to eat away at me, so I figured physically removing myself from Aberdeen Estates might help make her fade from my mind. You see, at that point, they had gotten engaged, and I knew it was futile to keep waiting."

Chloe nodded her understanding but was getting more and more uncomfortable by the minute as she watched the seriously sick dance Danny was doing back and forth between the two versions of his personality he had shown her.

"So you went abroad to try to let her go?" Chloe asked, prodding him along as he seemed to be lost in his memories.

"I did, but it was no good. I got busy and involved with my career, but I never met anyone who compared to Teresa. As hard as I tried, I could just not wipe her from my mind. Eventually, I realized that I needed to see her again and at least try to win her away from him."

Chloe shuddered again, seeing how that was likely to play out.

"So I came back to Green Pond with the story of it being partly a business trip and to see Jonathan again. What had transpired, you see, was much more than just an infatuation, Chloe. I really felt a deep love for Teresa that I just couldn't ignore any longer."

"Even though they were married and had children by this time?" Chloe asked.

"I was so focused on her that at the time, it didn't seem to matter. I told myself that Jonathan didn't deserve her based on how he had tossed me aside, and I was determined to prove that to her and win her over."

"Seems a long shot, Danny," Chloe said, "if you don't mind me saying so."

"That's okay. Yeah, I can see that now, but at the time, I was sure my plan would work."

"Not so much, huh?" she asked.

"Yeah, not so much. I bared my soul to her and told her exactly how I felt and how she had made a mistake marrying Jonathan—how a life with me traveling across Europe with the kids would be so much more exciting for her than being stuck in Green Pond."

He sighed and looked away again.

"I couldn't believe how harshly and quickly she

rebuffed me. I mean, it was like she didn't even consider my offer. In retrospect, I can see how ridiculous it was, but when you're in love…well, you often do things that aren't so rational and well-thought-out."

Just then, the new Danny came back, and the old Danny disappeared as Chloe looked on incredulously. This was not just a murderer who had acted impulsively due to jealousy of his brother's life with Teresa. Danny Thompson was a mentally disturbed man.

"She told me to leave her alone and never to speak to her again, or she would go to Jonathan and tell him everything. Knowing that, I couldn't have Jonathan privy to my attempt to steal away his wife as, on some level, his friendship and the bond we had experienced since we were kids was still very important to me."

"So you killed her instead?" Chloe asked.

"What choice did I have, Chloe? She would have ruined everything. Even if I had let her be, I had no guarantee that she wouldn't eventually go to Jonathan and tell him what I had tried to do."

Chloe now connected the feeling of paranoia that had come through in Teresa's diary entries as she was likely fearful that her turning Danny away so abruptly and without much empathy could make him consider hurting her in some way to make her sorry. If Danny had shown her any inkling of who he was now, Chloe could see where she might have become paranoid. Her writing might have become rambling, but it was not due to any overlying mental illness.

She could see her time running out as the story was obviously wrapping up. But she still had not come up with any reasonable plan to try for an escape. As long as she remained tied up, there just seemed to be no way out, and it was foolish to think Danny would untie her and Harold at some point before killing them and the kids. But Danny went on, oblivious to anything but his own narrative. Chloe guessed it might be the first time he had ever told anyone the actual story, and his narcissistic personality seemed to need an audience.

"So when Jonathan was away on business, I knew what I had to do. Right before he left, Jonathan and Teresa had had a very vocal and nasty argument. Something I knew was becoming more and more common between them. He was traveling more than she was comfortable with, and it finally came to a head. Everyone here—Reggie, Tony...even some gossips in town—knew of their troubles, and it was the perfect cover for me."

"You killed her and then tried to make it look like Jonathan had snapped after their last fight?"

"Very good, Chloe," Danny replied with a grin. "I knew you were bright. But even with all the pains and efforts I went to in setting the scene to make any reasonable person put the blame for her murder on Jonathan, the investigators finally said there just wasn't enough evidence to charge him."

"His alibi of being away too strong?"

"Apparently, it was the one factor I couldn't manipulate. He had multiple witnesses who put him far away from Green Pond at the time of her murder, and no links could be made showing he might have hired someone to kill her for him because it was me, you see."

Danny leaned back and exhaled as if it had required a huge emotional toll to finally get the whole story off his chest. Even as vile and despicable as the man was, Chloe figured anyone would feel the same if they had carried that secret around for so long.

"Anyway, Chloe," Danny went on, "enough of that. Storytime is over. Time to write the final chapter of this unfortunate situation and put my family's tragedy to rest once and for all."

Danny jumped from the cart, lifted Adam and Katie to their feet, and then set them next to the ATV. He then tied a short piece of rope between the restraints on her and Harold's wrists before slicing off the ties on their ankles. He walked them off the cart and put them beside the kids.

"Sorry about that, Chloe," Danny said as he got them down, "but I can't have you running off now, can I?"

Chloe looked over a few feet away from the ATV to see a very deep and seemingly bottomless cavity in the earth. The end was coming, and despite having tried her best to come up with a way to save them all, she saw it was not to be.

53

JULY 2008

*C*hloe wanted to fight back and resist Danny as he pulled them along toward the jagged opening, but she was so hopeless and feeling all her energy depleted after listening to Danny's horrid tale of murder and deception that she just gave up. As the aperture came closer and closer, Chloe figured it was likely Jonathan had already been dumped into the hole and that they were just to be added to the body count. Her last gesture of protest was to beg Danny to spare Adam and Katie.

"Please, Danny!" she pleaded, "Don't harm the kids! They're just innocent bystanders in all of this!"

"Sorry, Chloe," Danny replied with a cold, cutting edge to his voice, "but I can't risk leaving behind any loose ends before I leave the country. Just how it is."

Chloe felt tears coming to her eyes as she looked over and saw the children looking at her to save them. It was breaking her heart, but with Harold still out of it and both of them quite unable to break free and intervene, she looked away in shame and guilt. Danny pulled a revolver from the waistband of his jeans at the small of his back and aimed it at Harold.

"I'm not a complete savage, Chloe," Danny said bluntly. "It's not like I would just dump you down there still alive. Besides, you might find some way out, though, with the depth, that's unlikely. If only you had just done the jobs you had been hired for and stayed out of the family business."

Chloe clamped her eyes shut tightly, not wanting to have to witness Danny putting a bullet into Harold's head when all hell broke loose around them. With no warning, a huge gust of wind arose from the other side of the ATV, and the trees lashed back and forth in the gale. Danny lowered the revolver and looked up to see what was going on. The skies clouded over, and through a gap in the forest, an enormous whirlwind wound its way into the opening where they all stood.

Chloe looked that way and at once knew what was going on based on previous experiences; it had to be Teresa. The funnel came to a stop as Danny looked on incredulously as it began to turn a deep-red hue before taking on the human form of Teresa Thompson.

But unlike her last visit to them, this version was an angry and malevolent woman. Her laser stare was aimed directly at Danny as he stood open-mouthed, trying to get his brain to accept what his eyes were seeing. He just stood frozen in place and uttered a single word—"Teresa." A thin, crooked line of electricity sprang from the Teresa-thing's open palm and connected with the revolver, making Danny drop it as he screamed out in pain and clasped his injured hand to his chest with the other. He looked at her and began to babble.

"Teresa—how…I mean…you're…this can't be real! What are you?"

For the first time ever, Chloe heard an audible voice come from the apparition, and it was not so much spoken toward the cowering Danny as it was spewed with great emotion and hatred.

"*You bastard!*" the thing bellowed as the wind around her blew back her long blond hair. "*How dare you even consider doing anything like this to my children!*"

Chloe got Harold moving as she shuffled them toward the now-crying and near-hysterical Adam and Katie. She pulled Harold to his knees using the rope, tying them together before turning her attention to the kids.

"Adam! Katie! Come to me and get down!"

They went immediately and clung to her as best they could, considering all the restraints.

"Wait, Teresa!" Danny begged. "You don't understand!"

"*Quiet, you insolent worm! You come to me, professing your love, and then when it doesn't work out for you, this is your reaction? Not only do you kill the love of my life, but then you feel the need to add more innocent people to the tally just to cover it all up? Including two children? My two precious children!*"

Thunder and lightning covered the blackening skies as the Teresa-thing lolled her head back and looked straight overhead before emitting the most bloodcurdling and piercing scream of anguish and agony Chloe had ever heard in her life. She could feel the children trembling against her side as she pressed them between herself and Harold. Though she knew Teresa's intervention had saved them from Danny's sicked intentions, it was still a frightening and horrific scene to observe. But what she was going through was minor as she looked over to see Danny in shock and on the verge of going mad.

The Teresa-thing then floated over the ground, passing right through the ATV and the cart until she stood face to face with Danny. He fell to his knees and begged her for mercy with everything he had as tears poured from his eyes.

"Please, Teresa! I'm begging you. I was out of my mind just now! Please give me another chance!"

"You might be able to fool these good people, Danny, but in my plane of existence, I can see you for all that you are— what you've always been!"

Then with nothing more said, Chloe looked on as Teresa's apparition raised her arms as if a parishioner in a church asking for a divine blessing. Inexplicably, Danny's body began to rise from the ground as he screamed in terror, wildly flailing with his arms and kicking at the empty air below his feet.

"Teresa, please! For the love of God!" Danny bellowed.

"How dare *you invoke the name of God, you murderous shit!" she replied.*

He then gravitated sideways until he was directly over the black maw of the pit he had planned to use on

Chloe, Harold, and the kids. With a sudden vicious slash of lightning overhead, the Teresa-thing opened her fingers wide, and Danny's body dropped into the hole.

Chloe grimaced as she listened to his screams of desperation, helplessness, and terror as he fell and fell. Finally, his voice went silent, and the Teresa-thing lowered her arms to her sides. When all was quiet again, the skies cleared and the wind fell silent as Teresa turned toward Chloe, Harold, and her kids. The look of anger and vengeance had been replaced with one of appreciation and gratitude as she smiled at them. She looked to their bodies, and the restraints simply fell away as if they had never been tied tight in the first place. Chloe rubbed her wrists and then pulled the gags from Adam and Katie's mouths.

"You can talk to us?" Chloe asked.

"When need be, my dear. Normally, it's just more efficient and less troublesome to communicate by mind, like we did before. But with damaged souls like Danny, they're not deserving nor even evolved enough to make that an option. That make sense?"

Chloe nodded.

"But before I leave, let us continue in this manner."

"Thank you so much for saving us, Teresa. I tried as hard as I could, but it just didn't work out."

"You're very welcome, but there's no need to apologize. You and Harold were up against a formidable enemy. I know it looked hopeless there for you for a time, but I always had your backs. I just needed to wait until the right time to step in. You see, I can only materialize for short periods until I

need to...recharge, I guess, is the best way to explain it. Sorry if it was too traumatic."

"All is well now. I guess that's all that matters," Chloe replied.

"I need to go soon but know I'm always at your disposal if I'm needed, Chloe. One last thing?"

Chloe nodded.

"With Adam and Katie having no one to care for them now, there really is no extended family. I would like to entrust them to you and Harold...that is, if they agree to that."

Adam and Katie nodded madly as they looked to Chloe with anticipation in their eyes.

"Are you sure, Teresa?" Chloe asked.

"Absolutely. Do what you think is best. I know you have grown to love them like you were their real mother."

"Done," Chloe replied.

And with that, Teresa's human form disintegrated into a million minute particles and just blew away like dust across the forest in a mild breeze that had sprung up.

54

AUGUST 2008

*C*hloe and Harold pulled the kids close to them as the dust settled after Teresa's departure and soothed them until they seemed to have finally shaken off most of the ill effects of all that had gone on with Danny. They had no idea what Adam and Katie might be thinking or feeling at that moment. After all, they had just found out that their Uncle Danny had killed both their parents and had Teresa not stepped in, he would have added both of them to the list. Chloe had experienced some trauma in her own life, but in comparison, it paled to what these poor kids had endured if you added it all up.

But now was not the time to address their psyches, as cold as that felt to Chloe. That would come later and probably from a source much more capable and professionally trained in such matters than she and Harold were. Dr. Abrams came to mind. For now, she wiped their tear-stained faces and made sure they were at least physically intact after the rough incident with Danny.

"You guys, okay?" Chloe asked as she knelt down to their level.

They nodded numbly.

"I know this was a horrible thing for you," Chloe went on as she touched each of their faces with her open palm with tenderness, "but it's all over now. You're safe, okay?"

They smiled weakly and nodded again but said nothing. Chloe stood and turned to Harold, who was looking better but still not quite 100% himself, she thought.

"How about you, Harold?"

"I've been better, but for the most part, I'm okay."

"You can walk? Vision okay?"

He nodded and grinned. "Yeah...just one hell of a headache is all."

"Good. I guess first of all, before we get the kids taken care of, we need to wrap up this whole horrible episode in our lives."

"Police?" Harold asked.

"Yep...and it's a safe bet that including Teresa Thomson's help is out of the question. Any ideas on a good story to get us out of this mess?"

Harold sat with her next to the kids and pondered that for a few moments. "Well, let's look at what we have. We have Danny's confession over what really happened, and we actually saw him shoot this brother. And we have our abductions and then Danny's missing body."

"Not to mention that we have no idea where Jonathan's is."

"Good point…probably down that hole as well, but who knows for sure unless he left him back in the mansion."

"Based on Danny's plan, I can't believe he would just leave him lying dead to be found easily."

"How about this," Harold replied. "We contact the police and tell them the absolute truth up to and including our abductions here. Danny shot Jonathan at the mansion, and when we came to, we found ourselves out here, soon to be included in his rampage."

"Okay…so spill what Danny told us to explain it all, but then what? I mean, no Jonathan and no Danny to prove our story."

"Yeah, I know. Here's where some creativity is needed. My thought is to say that Danny lost his footing around that pit just as he was preparing to dump the kids and us into it. That we have no idea what became of Jonathan, though we suspect he might already be in the chasm as well."

"Then they can go excavating if they're so inclined to see if they can corroborate our story?"

"That was my thinking. What about Adam and Katie?"

Chloe nodded, realizing the police might want to interview them as well.

"I'm hoping that maybe their young ages might preclude that and that we can convince them that the incident was just too traumatic for them to have to relive it in interviews. Or maybe that they were blindfolded and didn't see anything. And of course, there's always the chance that they might mention that a ghost showed up to rescue us. My guess is that the police will see that as a child's creation to deal with the incident and just drop it."

"More likely, I think."

WITH THAT PLAN IN MIND, Harold got behind the wheel of the ATV and drove them back to the mansion, but in a much gentler and calmer manner than the trip out. Harold contacted the police, and they laid out their story just as they had decided back at the pit. Both Chloe and Harold were interrogated in separate interviews by a team of detectives, but in the end, they seemed satisfied with the explanation once they found the blood in the mansion from Jonathan's murder which Danny had not gotten around to cleaning up, and a visit out to the pit where Danny's body now lay. The detectives released them from any further inquiry and thankfully did not pursue any questioning of Adam and Katie, figuring the young children had been through enough and that they were unlikely to have anything of substance to add to the situation.

Detective Cantor, the lead investigator, told them they would eventually get some equipment out in the woods to excavate the pit, but that with evidence of clawing finger marks on the rim—Danny had futilely tried to save himself when Teresa had dropped him inside it—they were sure nothing more would be required of them. It seemed pretty cut and dry, he said, as to the veracity of their story.

"If anything unexpected comes up, we'll give you a call," Cantor said, "but realistically, consider your involvement in this case closed."

Harold and Chloe sighed with great relief when the police finally left after their final visit. The big question now was what would become of Adam and Katie. They had promised Teresa that they would make sure they were well-cared for, and Chloe had no intention of not fulfilling that promise.

"I know this is a big favor I'm about to ask of you, Harold," Chloe said, "but how would you feel if we looked into adopting them?"

Harold nodded thoughtfully, though he was sure this would be Chloe's natural inclination. And it was not like he had not had this thought as well. "What do you think our chances might be?" he asked her.

"From all we know, at least according to Teresa anyway, there's no extended family. I can see no reason she would lie about such a thing. After all they've been through, beginning with losing their mother, I can't imagine just walking away now and possibly having those sweet, somewhat psychologically bruised kids fall into the unknown of social services."

"I agree. The agencies do the best they can, but they have limited resources, and I'm afraid what might become of them without the professional care they will need to deal with what they've been through."

"With both Reggie and Tony as references to our connections with Adam and Katie since we've been here, I would say we have at least a better than fifty-fifty chance. Want to give it a try?"

Harold nodded, and then they called a lawyer in Green Pond recommended to them who dealt in adoption procedures and other custody protocols. Reggie and Tony did indeed step up and vouch for Harold and Chloe's character and dedication to the kids, even though it had been for just a short time. As well, pointing out that without them, the kids would likely end up in some foster home—and not necessarily the same one—which, in their opinion, might be a blow from which Adam and Katie might never recover.

Since she carried some weight and influence in town, Amanda Murray, the lawyer they had contacted, was able to cut through the normal layers of red tape and bureaucracy that an average adoption application required. She and Charles Baker, a judge she was on excellent terms with, set up a meeting that included everyone to discuss the application and make a decision. The judge's chambers were crowded with Harold, Chloe, Reggie, Tony, Adam, Katie, and Amanda. Baker reviewed the depositions that Reggie and Tony had made, as well as getting a first-hand account of Harold and Chloe's proposal plus how capable they were, both financially and emotionally, to take on two young children.

Amanda Murray offered a heartfelt and touching presentation for just how urgent and necessary it was that Adam and Katie be placed in a loving and caring environment versus a well-meaning, but often indifferent, social services effort. Harold and Chloe held their breath as Baker sat back and said nothing once Amanda was finished.

"Okay," Baker finally said as he pushed all the paperwork aside. "Just one more thing, I guess, before I make a decision. Adam? Katie?"

The children looked up at the judge.

"Do you understand what is being proposed here, kids?"

They nodded.

"How do you feel about going to live with Harold and Chloe?"

Both their faces lit up with wide smiles.

"For real?" Adam asked.

"For real, son," Baker replied.

"Oh, yes," they both replied almost as one.

The judge smiled, and the room laughed lightly, appreciating his final requirement to move forward. "That's all I need," Baker said as he signed off on all the necessary paperwork. "It will take a few days for this to get processed, but as of now, consider it a done deal."

Adam and Katie fled to Harold and Katie, and there was not a dry eye in the room.

55

SEPTEMBER 2008

*H*arold and Chloe were finally back in Hampton after a long and surprising adventure in Green Pond. They had gone there to heal Chloe from their recent loss and had come back with the full family they had always dreamed of. It had not been easy, and there had been adjustments, but overall, life was good at Case de Reynolds. Dr. Abrams did indeed work with Adam and Katie to help them deal with all they had gone through back in Green Pond, and the kids enrolled in the public school system there based on her recommendation that it would add to their overall recovery.

"Being isolated and away from children their own ages is not a good idea," she told Harold and Chloe after one session. "They need to interact with their peers to help them fully adapt to this new life."

And so they did. Meanwhile, back in Green Pond, Aberdeen Estates went shuttered once again as it had been before Jonathan and Teresa Thompson had purchased the place. When the story of Danny Thompson became public knowledge, the old mansion was widely avoided, and multiple realtors finally gave up when there was simply no one anywhere who had even the slightest interest in buying the home. Wild stories and legend soon sprang up, fueled by people like Roger Yardley, no doubt, that the place was cursed and possibly haunted. It became especially poignant around Halloween when tales of the legacy of Aberdeen Estates were used to both entertain and frighten children of all ages.

The one positive result from the fallout, if there were one, in Green Pond and the mansion, was that Green Pond slowly became a tourist draw for the curious, especially those having a keen interest in the paranormal. One of the myriad of cable shows focusing on such things, *Mysteries of the Other Side*, even did a piece on it for one of their shows. The title "The Aberdeen Estates Horror" was a bit over the top for most residents, but none of the merchants in town ever complained about how much new business they were getting from it all. After all, who does not love a good local legend?

Sign up for new release updates and receive your free copy of "Missed Connections: A Small town Mystery", Free Audible codes, and deep discounts on new releases! Click Here

Check out the complete Haunted House Series! Click Here!